To my two sons, J. W. and Eric, who were the catalyst for the formation of the characters and advetures. Without them I would not have had the desire to create this manuscript. I wish to thank them for their inspiration and their confidence in me to put these stories on paper for their future use in entertaining their children. Together we have developed memories that will hopefully last several generations.

ACKNOWLEDGMENTS

I want to extend my deepest gratitude to those who have helped me achieve this publication, my first book. Again I acknowledge my sons, for without them, I would have never begun telling stories. My most sincere thanks go to my wife, Barbara, for supporting me in my efforts. Needless to say, the time and dedication committed to this book left many neglected household projects waiting in the background. My wife, while she could have complained, knew how important this task was, not only to me but to our children. May she remain equally patient in my future endeavors.

Others who have been instrumental in this achievement are: Caryn Hill, whose overabundance of energy and enthusiasm pushed me to finish the writing and get it to market, my great nephew, Luke Ruther, who read and proofed the work from his age perspective. Through his pointed suggestions, the work was marvelously enhanced. Additionally, I owe a great deal of appreciation to Todd Brausch, the gifted artist who brings the story to life through his breathtaking illustrations; Tim Brausch and Shannon Prinzo, who graciously volunteered their time in proofing the finished transcript for all the blunders and errors that escaped me; all the relatives and friends who read the work from an adult perspective and offered their critiques so as to provide a more enjoyable experience for readers of all ages. Finally, I owe a lifetime of gratitude to God for imbedding in me a vivid and active imagination, as well as the drive to see this book to fruition. A final thanks goes to you, the readers. Without you, this work is no more than ink on paper.

Thank you all! Your amazing support has helped to produce a product I hope will be enjoyed by many people for many years to come. I love you all. You are in my thoughts every time I lift a copy.

PREFACE

Many years ago, when my children were young, I was away more than I was home. I had a burning desire to spend quality time with my two boys, and so it evolved that I would be the parent who provided bedtime stories. They would climb up on my lap and listen to the array of standard children's books our miniscule library held. Before I knew it, we had read all of the available stories.

Several rotations of the same books became laborious, even monotonous. To combat the decline of enthusiasm, and the ruin of what little time I had to share with my sons, I started to mix and match the stories. *Little Red Riding Hood* was inserted into the tale of *The Three Little Pigs,* and Jack was replaced by Goldilocks in *Jack and the Bean Stalk.* Although this was humorous, the children found themselves compelled to correct my obvious errors. The end result was more akin to a pep talk for playtime rather than the desired prelude to sleep.

My new strategy was to tell them stories of my own making. Thus, *The Kingdom of Mangonel* was born. They loved the mini-adventures I took them on and went to bed happy. Years passed. Eventually, one of my sons requested that I put those old stories on paper for him to read to his children someday. At first I rejected the idea, but several requests later convinced me of the sincerity of his plea, culminating in this book.

I designed these stories to be read over a long period of time. One chapter per night seems a good pace. More than a few days between readings can foster a loss of continuity and may contribute to a diminished interest, not only in this story but in reading in general. Additionally, this tome contains some fundamental lessons in life. I encourage you to seek them out, perhaps during a second reading.

I encourage you, the reader, to let your mind wander and immerse yourselves into the fantasy world I have attempted to create. Should you discover the pleasures of reading along the way, I hope you don't stop at this little dunking but rather leap into the river of available books and go for a healthy swim!

It's my wish that while reading this story, the child, parent, aunt, uncle, or grandparent will use the dictionaries provided at the end of each chapter. For the younger readers, they may prove to be a tool to increase vocabulary, while the adults may find them useful should they require a quick reference.

CONTENTS

CHAPTER 1

Discovering the Kingdom of Mangonel

Buddy Bailey, a young boy growing up in Boulder, Colorado, dreamed that someday he would leave his home for a more exciting life. He loved the great outdoors and the adventures he found when not at home or in school. For now, however, he had to be satisfied with the life he had. His childhood had been difficult. His father had passed away before he was born. This left him and his mother to fend for themselves.

Alexander Bailey, Buddy's father, had come home from the army as soon as he had finished his duty stint in the Philippines. Everything in Alexander's life seemed to be coming together. The house was in good shape, he had a new job, and shortly after his return, his wife, Betty, became pregnant with Buddy, their soon-to-be new son. However, Alexander would never see his son. After being home from the service for only a few months, Alexander fell terribly ill. He had contracted an unusual strain of malaria that somehow had gone undetected. The disease was relentless, and five days after the New Year, he passed away.

Buddy Bailey was born in July of that year. Ten years passed while he and his mother maintained the house in Boulder as best they could. For Buddy, the pressures of being the man of the house so early in life caused him to grow up faster than any of the other children he knew. Because of the necessary demands placed on him, most of the other children his age seemed rather childish, and his preference for being alone was misinterpreted as being shy or backward.

Buddy's home was at the edge of the city limits, with the back of their property abutting a large park. The great outdoors and numerous adventures awaited him in those woods. It was quiet there. Paths wound in, out, and around the trees that filled the eighteen hundred–acre public park that lay just on the other side of the backyard fence. Buddy's countless adventures had placed him on many of those trails.

One warm day in June, just one month before his eleventh birthday, Buddy awoke feeling ready for almost anything. The winter had been long, and he looked forward to his first excursion of the year in his most favorite place—the park. In addition to the park, Buddy loved his book on grizzly bears, and he cherished his father's old army backpack. His father had drawn a castle on the back of the pack in reference to their last name, Bailey (a courtyard inside the outermost walls of a castle). The book about grizzly bears was one he had read several times, but he never tired of it. He had a habit of taking the book and backpack nearly everywhere he went. Having the backpack always felt like he had his dad hugging him, an added benefit to the fact that it allowed him to comfortably carry everything he needed for the day.

To Buddy, grizzlies were the greatest animals on earth. They are the kings of the mountains, much like the lion is the king of the jungle. Buddy wished someday he could experience that sort of freedom—that sort of power.

Having the park behind his house was like having his very own private land of adventure right out his back door. All he had to do was cross over the fence his father had built to keep the park visitors out, and he was off to who-knew-where.

On that day, Buddy stuffed his favorite book inside the pack, along with a water jar, a few crackers, and a couple of other snacks before he started out to see what the park might have in store for him. He felt he was ready for a good adventure, and was prepared to go anywhere his imagination wanted to carry him. He didn't care, as long as he was out and about. In the past, he had imagined he was in Africa on a hunt for a wild and dangerous animal; he had sailed the vast Pacific Ocean to an undiscovered island; he had been to an alligator-infested swamp; and he had visited so many other places he couldn't keep track of them all.

On this particular day, Buddy had a difficult time coming up with anything exciting to do. While strolling along one of the paths he was sure he had been on before, he caught a glimpse of something from the corner of his eye. Turning to face the object, he saw the most unusual bush he had ever come across. The bush was heavy with shiny black and stark white leaves. There were so many leaves the branches weren't growing up any longer; instead, they were bent over so far that they touched the earth. When Buddy stood back and looked at the bush, he thought it resembled the top of an opened umbrella resting on the ground. He went up to the plant where there was a small break in the foliage. Peering through that opening, he noticed that under all those leaves was a large vacant space, just like the big umbrella he had pictured in his mind. He crawled under the leaves and sat with his back against the base of the plant. This was a perfect place to quietly read his favorite book.

As Buddy read his book about grizzly bears, he found himself thinking of what it might be like to be a bear. How wonderful it would be to roam the mountain forests and never be afraid, because as a grizzly, he would be the one in charge; he would be the king of the mountain. He thought, *Wouldn't that be wonderful? No more city smog and noise. No more rules to follow, and no more chores to do.* Then he sort of mumbled to himself, "I wish I could be a grizzly bear, even if only for a short time."

Almost immediately, Buddy began to feel strange. His stomach began to feel jittery. His fingers and toes felt like they had fallen asleep. His head ached. His skin felt like it was full of goose bumps. He looked at his hands and saw they were changing. There was a lot of hair growing all over his body. His fingers were starting to look like paws. His nose and mouth really hurt, and when he reached up to touch them, he found they were turning into a snout. Buddy became so frightened, he fainted.

Later, he awoke from his faint. By now he had completely transformed into a bear cub. He was still under the bush, but he was now faced with what he was going to tell his mother when he got home. He tried to wish himself back to being a boy, but he remained a bear. Knowing there was nothing to do but to go home and tell his mother what had happened, he spread the leaves of the unusual bush and climbed out from underneath it.

Much to his surprise, he found himself staring at a landscape that he knew was not in his favorite park. He was confused and disoriented. What had happened? Where was he?

Looking around, Buddy saw that this place was not at all like his home. The ground was a different color, the trees had square trunks, the sky was a darker blue, and the air smelled cleaner than at his home near the city. Suddenly he missed home very much. He thought of his mother and hoped she wouldn't be too worried about him. By now he knew he was far from home. He was frightened, and he desperately wanted to find his way back to the park.

"I want to go back home," he said with a sigh. Then in an even quieter voice he mumbled, "I'm sorry I ever wanted to be a bear. I wish I could go back home."

Buddy sat down and cried. Soon he realized that crying was not going to change anything. He was the man in his house back in Colorado. He needed to pull himself together. He needed to do something about the situation. He threw his shoulders back and vowed he would find his way home, no matter what.

All the excitement made the little bear cub hungry. "Sure wish I could get something to eat around here," he muttered. He began to pace around the bush and ran smack into a smaller plant full of fat, ripe berries. Buddy happily ate as many as he could, yet there were plenty left. It was as if the berries grew back as fast as he could eat them. With his belly full, he thought, *Being a bear might not be so bad after all.*

No longer hungry, he took some time to survey the land. Having never been here before, he needed to see where he was to determine which way he should go to get back home. Off to one side, just beyond a few small trees, he could see a large open field. On the opposite side of the field there was nothing but trees. He couldn't see what was behind him because of the forest he was standing in, so he marched into the big field, turned back around, and there in the distance, peeking above the forest, were mountains. Buddy decided it would be best if he headed in that direction. His home had to be somewhere in that mountain range. It was going to be a long hike, but walking was a good thing; it gave him something to concentrate on as he began working his way deeper into the forest that stood between him and what he thought was home.

The more Buddy walked, the farther away the mountains seemed to be. The trees were tall, with thick trunks, and the many fallen branches made his progress slow. Day turned to evening; evening turned to night. The trees blocked the light of the stars and moon, making it very dark in the forest. The little grizzly curled up next to an old tree. He fell asleep wishing that the mountains were not so far away.

The next morning, Buddy awoke, found more berries to eat, and then climbed a big tree to get his bearings. From the top branches, he was able to look all around. Today the mountains looked to be much closer. It must have been the dark sky playing tricks on him last night, or maybe he had walked a great deal farther than he thought. He figured he would be at the bottom of the mountains in just a few hours, but he knew that distant mountains can play tricks on your judgment. The idea of being home made him very happy. His walk that morning was brisk, and he whistled his favorite song while he picked his way through the trees.

Slowly, the trees changed from one type to another. The tall oak and maple-like trees were replaced by more and more trees that resembled pine trees. Then, without noticing the gradual change, Buddy became aware that the broad-leafed trees were behind him and all the needle-leafed trees in front of him. This area was much easier for hiking, as there were fewer fallen tree limbs and the ground was covered with a soft carpet of pine needles.

Around noon Buddy grew tired. A little frustrated, he said with a sigh, "I sure wish those mountains were not so far away."

From nowhere came a deep, raspy voice. "Why are you wishing?" Buddy jumped and spun around to see who was talking to him. He was crouched down, close to the ground, ready to defend himself, but nobody was there.

"Who said that? Where are you?" Buddy asked. "Come out so I can see you," he shouted.

"Who am I?" asked the voice. "I am one of the many who make this forest. My name is Dex-exerankinter, but you may call me Dex. Where am I? You are standing beneath me," the voice answered. "Now it is time for you to tell me who you are."

Buddy couldn't see anyone, so he remained in his defensive position. Still, he answered as calmly as he could, "I am Buddy." Not really sure of what to say next, he finished with, "Um … er, I'm Buddy, Buddy Bailey from Colorado. I wished to be a bear, fell asleep under a bush, and woke up here. I know that sounds strange, but that's the truth."

"Not strange at all," replied the voice from nowhere. "People arrive here in many different ways but not often through the sort of passage you describe."

"Where am I?" Buddy inquired. "Can you tell me what has happened? How do I get home? And again, where are you?"

"Oh, my apologies," came Dex's voice from nowhere. "I am a talking tree in this Forest of Talking Trees. Not all of the trees in the forest can speak, but many can. Please turn around; your back is to me." Buddy did as he was asked. "You wish to know where you are. You are in the kingdom of Mangonel, within the Forest of the Talking Trees. You obviously know how you got here, but the going home is not so easy."

Buddy thought it was odd to see a tree talking to a bear but soon got used to it. At that exact moment, he realized it was just as odd for a bear to be speaking to a tree. Dex and Buddy talked for a while. Buddy told the tree what had happened to him, and Dex told Buddy a little about the kingdom of Mangonel.

Dex-exerankinter explained, "Wishing to be a bear is not acceptable on earth, so when your wish came true, you were sent here, to Mangonel, where any number of wonders takes place. The kingdom of Mangonel is over, under, and around your world, all at the same time. Mangonel is alongside every place on earth, and the people have no idea it exists. This place is populated by earth people and animals. Some come to us through walkways, some through waterways, and like you, some through wishes. You told me when you arrived you were hungry and found a bush with never-ending fruit. That happened only because you made a wish. You see, you arrived in the land of the wishing trees. Didn't you notice that everything you wished for came true?"

"No, I did not," said Buddy a bit angrily. "In fact, I wished to go back home and that didn't happen."

The tree laughed like all trees laugh, and its branches wiggled and pine needles swayed. "Ha, ha, ha, ha, you are a silly one," said the tree. "You cannot un-wish something. That would be like eating and wishing you hadn't. The food is already gone and in your belly. It is like when you say something you wish you hadn't. You cannot take it back by wishing. You must be careful what you wish for because nearly always there is a price to pay when it is granted." Dex continued with its explanation of Mangonel. "In Mangonel you will experience many strange places and odd occurrences. Be prepared for peculiarities because here they are normal. Occasionally you may find a wishing tree growing outside the Wishing Forest. Also, there are magnificent wandering-talking trees, like myself.

"Many people from many places have come to Mangonel. Once here, they make their home here. Each group has claimed a part of the land and developed it to suit their particular style of living. You, as a traveler, must remember you are the visitor."

When the tree had finished, Buddy thanked him for the advice, and because there were so many tall trees that blocked his view, he asked which direction he should go to get to the mountains. Dex rustled his branches. "You must go to the sun in the morning and away from it in the afternoon. Depending on your progress, you should reach the bottom of the nearest mountains around this time tomorrow. It is very hard for a tree to judge time; we travel much slower than you."

Then, just as Buddy was about to leave, Dex called him back. The kind tree offered one last bit of advice. "Whenever you speak to a talking tree, you must be careful. Not all trees tell the truth. You are lucky; I am a truthful tree." At this point, Buddy wasn't sure he should trust this tree or any tree. Dex could see Buddy was skeptical. "Remember, I am also a wandering tree, so we may meet again. Wandering trees never lie. We are afraid that in the future we may come across the person we lied to. Should that happen, the one we offended might put an end to the lies by cutting us down. All the other stationary talking trees believe a traveler will never return, so sometimes they don't tell the truth. You can always trust a wandering-talking tree."

Buddy thanked the tree for his advice. As he turned to leave, the tree called out once again, "Be safe on your journey, little bear. It was nice meeting you. I hope to see you again sometime."

Dictionary—Chapter 1

Abut: *To touch or be alongside one side of something*

Apology: *To express or say you are sorry*

Cherish: *To feel or show great love for somebody or something*

Concentrate: *To focus all your thoughts on one subject or activity*

Contracted: *Caught or developed an illness or disease*

Crouch: *To squat down close to the ground, waiting to spring or run forward*

Defensive: *Concentrating on preventing an opponent from gaining an advantage*

Desperately: *Wanting or needing something very much*

Determine: *To decide on something or to find out something*

Developed: *Made into a residential, urban area, like a town*

Discharged: *Relieved of duty service, as in the army, navy, air force, or marines*

Disoriented: *To feel lost or confused, especially with regard to direction or position*

Excursion: *A short trip*

Foliage: *The leaves of a plant or tree*

Frustrated: *Not feeling satisfied with an outcome*

Glimpse: *A quick or incomplete look at somebody or something*

Judgment: *An opinion or decision obtained through logic*

Magnificent: *Beautiful and impressive*

Malaria: *An infectious disease caused by a parasite, like mosquitoes, common in tropics*

Misinterpreted: *Did not understand the proper meaning of something*

Occasionally: *Sometimes but not regularly or often*

Occurrence: *The act of something happening or something that has happened*

Peculiar: *Odd or unusual*

Philippines: *A group of islands in the South Pacific*

Preference: *The more desirable choice of view or course of action*

Relentless: *Never slackening but continuing always at the same intense, demanding level*

Resemble: *To be similar to somebody or something*

Situation: *What is happening in a particular place or time*

Snout: *The projecting part of the head, consisting of nose and mouth*

Stint: *Time, turn, shift*

Survey: *To look at or consider something in a general or very broad way*

Transform: *To change somebody or something completely,*

Undetected: *Hidden, unnoticed, concealed*

Vow: *A solemn promise*

CHAPTER 2

Buddy and the Cave of Wonders

After speaking with Dex, the wandering-talking tree, and getting a great deal of information he did not yet understand, Buddy continued heading away from the sun, just as he was instructed. Suddenly, for no apparent reason, he found himself searching for his backpack. It was missing, and so were all of the provisions he had jammed inside. Recalling what had taken place, he knew the pack didn't make the journey to the kingdom of Mangonel. His only possession from earth was probably still under the strange bush back in Colorado where nobody would find it. He missed not having it with him as much as he missed home.

By now it was getting late in the day. The sky was turning gray, not just because it was dusk but also because rain clouds were forming overhead. Rain … just what he needed. The thought of rain put Buddy in a bad mood. The last two days had been terrible, and now, with night coming on, he was going to have to sleep in the rain. He tried wishing for some shelter, but there weren't any wishing trees around. He couldn't find anyplace cozy to rest, so he called out to the forest to see if any talking trees were nearby to give him some advice, but there was no response. Buddy continued walking until it got dark. He curled up near some small trees, covered himself with pine needles, and restlessly fell asleep.

He didn't get much rest that night. The trees and the pine needles didn't do much to keep him warm or dry. He was cold, wet, and scared. For breakfast he ate some pine nuts. Bears eat these sometimes. He was happy to have them, and there were plenty lying about. *Let's see now*, Buddy thought. *It is morning, so I am supposed to walk to the sun.* He looked up at the sky, but the dark clouds shielded the sun's rays. He wasn't sure which way to go. The rain washed away his tracks from the night before, so he couldn't establish a direction from yesterday's footprints. There was just no way of telling which way he had to travel. Climbing one of the tall trees, he was able see all around. As he looked about, he couldn't miss the mountains. They were very large and very close. Buddy was relieved that he had reestablished a direction to follow. Not knowing which way to go is very scary. He would have to remember to set his bearings from now on. He could mark a tree, bend a branch, line up some stones, or scratch the ground to show which route he was to take the next day.

By the time Buddy got back to the ground, he was all mixed up again, so he just took his best guess and started walking. He had already entered the thickest part of the forest, making his progress very slow. The sunlight was still blocked by the thick clouds and the branches of the many trees that surrounded him. Buddy let out a long breath and asked himself, "Which way now?"

"That way," offered a deep, mellow voice.

Startled, Buddy once again crouched down, preparing to defend himself. Not seeing anyone, he asked, "Are you a talking tree?" He paused, and then trying to get some response, he called out, "Could you show me which way to go again?"

"Sure, and yes, I am a talking tree. I am Zib-awgerkaztin, at your service. The mountains are that way," and a branch of a tree swayed, sort of pointing in one direction.

"Nice to meet you, Zid; I am Buddy Bear."

"*Zid*!" screamed the tree. "How dare you. I told you my name, and I would appreciate you using it."

"Okay, Mr. Zib-angrystinkerman," said Buddy.

"*No, no, no,* it is Zib-awgerkaztin, not—whatever you said."

"All right, Zib-agerkatsin, and thank you kindly for your advice," came from Buddy's mouth, but before the tree could complain again, Buddy remembered the advice of Dex, the wandering-talking tree. He had said not to trust all talking trees, so to be sure, Buddy asked again, "Which way, and by the way, are you a wandering tree?"

16

The answer came with a harsh tone. "How dare you! I most certainly am a wandering tree, and the direction I gave you is just as I have stated before. You must go that way." This time a totally different limb shook and pointed in a completely different direction. Buddy knew this was not a wandering tree and most certainly was not a truthful one.

Buddy began walking. He was going to take his original course when the tree shouted, "Hey, I told you to go that way," and all the branches shook and swayed at the same time.

"Okay, then I will go that way," replied Buddy. He shook himself all over like the tree had done, and kept right on walking.

"That's better," said the tree. "Next time, if you are not going to take the advice given, don't ask for it."

Buddy, knowing the tree was lying, moved on in the direction he had chosen. He felt good about not being fooled.

When he climbed the tall tree, he had seen that the mountains were close, but it was taking him too long to get there. Hours passed, and still there were no mountains. The trees were no help. They all looked the same to him. Without the sun to tell the direction, Buddy was in a fix.

"What are you doing here?" a familiar voice questioned. "I told you to go that way," and there was a rustling of tree branches. Buddy had traveled in a big circle.

Another voice entered the conversation. This one was female, "Don't tell him that. He will be lost forever if he listens to you." Then the two trees started arguing while Buddy stood and listened.

"Be quiet. I know my way around the forest," snarled Zib-awgerkaztin.

"How could you? All you do is stay in one place."

"Yes, but I have been here for a very long time. I have known this forest since I was a seedling."

"Granted, but you only know this spot where you are growing," said the new tree. "Can you tell me the way to—let's see, Balloon Billy's or Fairy Lake?"

"Who is Balloon Billy?" asked Zib.

With a tone of finality, the lady tree ended the argument. "No use for further discussion. My point has been made.

"Now, young bear, where are you trying to go? I am a wandering tree, as you may have guessed. I am called Angelindervood. I have roamed all of Mangonel and can assist you in finding wherever you seek."

"Thank you," came out in a sigh. "How do I find the mountains?"

"The mountains, you say. The peaks of the Major Mountains lie due east from where you stand. The West Mountains are due south, and the East Mountains are southeast. Which do you want?"

This was very confusing. Buddy had been traveling to the sun, so he asked, "Which mountains will I find if I travel to the sun in the morning, and away from the sun in the afternoon?"

Angelindervood was quick with her answer. "The sun rises in the east and sets in the west. If you go toward the sun in the morning, you are going east. If you go away from the sun in the afternoon, east is still in front of you, while west remains behind you. That would mean you were heading to the Major Mountains." A branch shook as it pointed out a single direction. "You will come to the bottom of the Major Mountain range in just a few hours if you go that way." Just then the sun came through the clouds. The bright sun was proof that the tree was telling the truth.

"You were a big help," said Buddy. "I hope to see you again sometime, Miss Angelindervood."

"Perhaps," the tree said with a sigh, "perhaps!"

Having a plan to follow, the bear cub started off again. This time he was going in the right direction, and the sun was up to help guide him on his way.

In a few hours, he was standing at the bottom of some very tall mountains. He knew they were high because it was warm where he was, but the peaks were covered in snow. It is always cold on high mountains. The snow never melts on the highest ones.

Buddy's next challenge was to climb the steep slopes. He knew he wouldn't find his home in this mountain range. He was in a different world altogether. Dex, the talking tree, told him he had arrived in the kingdom of Mangonel, but his home was in Colorado.

Buddy picked out a spot high up on the mountainside that looked like there could be a pathway going over the top. Although he didn't know what was on the other side, he was willing to go there just to find out. Left paws first, then the right, left, right, left, right. He was on his way.

It was easy going for a while, but then the rocks got bigger, and the climb got steeper, and steeper, and steeper. Higher and higher he climbed. The air became thinner the higher he went. That is to say there was less oxygen in the air. He could feel the difference in his lungs. His breaths came in short pants. The lesser oxygen made him feel dizzy. However, this was not too bothersome for him. He knew he would get used to it soon. After all, he was born near the mountains.

Nighttime came, but Buddy was still high in the mountains. A large boulder with an overhanging edge made a great temporary home for a bear looking for a place to spend the night. The beehive he found nearby was an added benefit, and it was loaded with sweet honey. There was even some honey left over for breakfast the next morning. He slept well that night and woke up to see some frost on the ground. Being a bear, Buddy got the idea it might be time to hibernate, but the boy in him knew it wasn't winter. He also knew this was no time to go to sleep if he was going to ever find his way back home.

Winding mountain paths led him higher still and closer to the spot he had picked out way down at the base of the cliff. Then, as he turned a corner and pushed a sticker bush out of his way, he saw the dark entrance of a cave. He couldn't stop himself from going nearer to the opening. As he approached the mouth of the cave, he felt a breeze coming from the gaping hole. A strange sound was being carried along by the breeze. It sounded like soft music. Then too, it also sounded like someone speaking—no, maybe a whistle. No, maybe more like a hum. What was it?

Buddy called into the cave, "Hello!" He paused and tried again, louder this time. "Hellooooo! Is anyone in there?"

The whistling, humming music stopped and then started again. It sounded like, "Eeeeeloooo." Then it continued to blow. More wordlike noises were formed. "Oouuuu errrrrr oouuuu?" The words were long, drawn out, and hard to understand.

Buddy thought and thought while listening to the soft musical tones coming from the cave. It was time for him to try again. "Is someone in the cave?" he shouted.

"Eeeeeyyyyyyyeeeeessssssssssss," sounded pretty clear. Buddy was now sure someone was in there. "Cuuuuummmmmm nnnnnnnnn brrrrrrr," finished the voice.

It was sounding more like words each time. The cave person had said, "Yes, come in, bear." While he tried to get this all sorted out in his head, the cave person spoke again. "Iiiiiiiiiiiyeeeee wheeeeel nnnnut urt ouu." That sounded like, "I will not hurt you," but Buddy wasn't absolutely sure. It was slowly getting easier to understand the breezy voice, so Buddy sat near the cave opening and waited for more noises to come from inside.

The next time the humming, whistling music came, it was soft but very clear. It still sounded like music to Buddy as it traveled along in the breeze. "Come into my cave where it is warm. I will not hurt you. I am Ryla of the Wind. You are at my Cave of Wonders. I hide in here to give Mangonel nice days. When I get upset, I come out of the cave. That is when I cause everything, from a gentle breeze to a swirling tornado." Buddy was soothed by the voice but alarmed that Ryla could cause such terrible storms as tornados.

Timidly, Buddy entered the cave but only just a little. The warm breeze felt good. "I cannot see you. Is everyone in Mangonel invisible? Where are you, exactly? Furthermore, if you are the wind, how can you speak to me?"

"Silly little bear, nobody can see the wind. I am anywhere I wish to be in Mangonel, anytime I please. No one can control me; I am Ryla. I am the wind. I speak to you by blowing across the stalactites and stalagmites deep in this cave. I can choose which ones to blow across to make sounds, and the tones I make connect to form words that you can understand." Buddy thought this was a pretty neat trick.

"I know many things because I have been here in the kingdom of Mangonel since the very beginning. Over time, I have traveled to every place in Mangonel and far beyond the limits of the kingdom. I have learned how people make fire, how they build things, where they live, how they live, and a great deal more. I can teach you much if you will keep me company. I am powerful, but I am lonely," Ryla explained.

Buddy listened and learned. He stayed all night and learned everything Ryla was willing to teach him. Ryla told him of the different people living in Mangonel. She described the land to him while she used little whirlwinds to form a map on the dusty cave floor for Buddy to see. Buddy spoke of his mother, his home in Colorado, and how he arrived in Mangonel. The rest of the evening was spent in pleasant conversation. Even though he couldn't see Ryla, it was nice having company. When it was very late, Ryla told Buddy he should go to sleep because she was going out to roam the countryside. There were some towns that needed a cool breeze, and the I-Mees needed a nasty blast.

As Buddy drifted off to sleep, he could hear Ryla whispering, "Goodnight, Buddy, goooood niiiiiiii. Goooooooooooooooooooooo nnnnnnnnnnnnnnnnnnnnnn-niiiiiiiiiiiiiiiii." As she left the cave, her voice became less and less clear until it became just a little breeze again.

Dictionary —Chapter 2

Alarmed: *Afraid, frightened*

Apparent: *Clearly seen or understood*

Appreciation: *A feeling of gratitude*

Bearings: *A known compass direction used for finding a predetermined destination*

Benefit: *Something that has a good effect*

Boulder: *A large rock*

Confusing: *Difficult to understand, unclear*

Conversation: *The activity of talking with somebody*

Course: *Direction or route*

Described: *To give details or characteristics of something or someone*

Finality: *The last thing; the end.*

Hibernate: *To be dormant, sleep through a long period of time*

Instruct: *Teach somebody how to do something*

Journey: *A trip*

Mellow: *Warm, soft, and comforting*

Original: *First to exist*

Overhanging: *Something that extends over and beyond, leaving a sheltered space*

Oxygen: *The air we breathe; colorless, odorless gas essential for plant and human life*

Provisions: *Supplies of food and other necessities, especially for a journey*

Reestablished: *Noted and recognized something for second time*

Relieved: *A temporary break from something unpleasant*

Seedling: *A young plant that has been grown from a seed.*

Shielded: *Protected*

Snarl: *To speak or say something angrily.*

Stalactite: *A pillar of limestone hanging from a cave's roof*

Stalagmite: *A pillar of limestone that has formed from a cave's floor*

Surround: *To occupy the space all around something*

Temporary: *Lasting only a short time*

Timidity: *Lack of courage or self-assurance*

Tornado: *Very destructive, funnel-shaped, rotating column of wind*

CHAPTER 3

Balloon Billy

Ryla of the Wind allowed Buddy to sleep in her cave while she went out roaming the countryside. She also gave him a great deal of advice and knowledge. The map she had drawn on the cave floor had to be committed to memory, but Buddy thought he could remember a pretty good amount of it. He slept better that night than he had in days. The next morning he awoke refreshed and ready to go.

Calling to Ryla to express his thanks and to say good-bye did no good. When he looked outside the cave, he knew why. Ryla was already out making gusts of wind over and through the mountain range. He called his good-bye once more in the hope that she would hear. He was fairly sure he heard, "You are welcome. Be safe, little bear," whispered in the air.

Leaving the cave, he continued east on his journey. He crossed over the mountains' highest peak and began his descent. Going downhill was a lot easier than climbing. Buddy decided to go to the base of the peaks at the edge of the desert. From there he turned south, where he hoped to find Mr. Balloon Billy, the person Angelindevood, the talking tree, had mentioned. Ryla had told him that Mr. Billy lived high up on the east side of the mountains and south of the Cave of Wonders. She also said Balloon Billy might be able to help him on his way by floating him over Mangonel in his giant flying balloon. Buddy had never seen a giant flying balloon before and was very curious. He also wanted to know how this balloon could help him get home.

Down the mountain Buddy went, being very careful not to fall. He couldn't rely on a wishing tree being near to stop a tumble or to grant a wish to cure any injuries. If he stumbled here, he could break a leg or something. He was a very lucky bear that day as he climbed over boulders, around hills, through the trees, and across streams. At one stream he caught a few fish. He ate some and saved some for his dinner. Catching fish took a long time because he was not very good at fishing. Then, as Buddy descended, the weather got warmer. The warm sun felt good and turned that day's journey into a pleasant walk.

As he got closer to the base of the mountains and approached the desert floor, the temperature became downright hot. He had seen the desert to the east while coming down the mountain. He didn't want to venture into that desolate furnace if he could avoid it. At the base of the mountains, he had turned south because that was where Ryla said Mr. Billy lived. Going south placed the morning sun on Buddy's left side and the mountain range on his right. All he needed to do was stay close to the cliffs. This would keep him safe from the desert, while at the same time, he would eventually come across Mr. Balloon Billy's home.

The heat from the sun baking on the white desert sand made Buddy very tired. He was unable to walk as fast as he did on the cooler paths in the mountains. There were no trees to his left. The hot sun baked down on him all morning, and when the sun went over the mountains, it quickly became very cold. All he wanted to do was find some place to curl up and take a nap. Since he had no place to go, and nobody was expecting him, that is just what he did. He found a comfortable spot to rest and went to sleep.

The next day was just like the last, early sunrise, hot, dry morning, very hot noontime, and a cold afternoon and night. He traveled for five days like this, napping many times during his walk south. Every day was like the last. He didn't go very fast, and neither did he go very far. His lethargy turned what could have been two days of travel into a long trip.

To Buddy, it seemed like he had gone a great distance. He was afraid he had passed by Mr. Balloon Billy's. At a little fork in the path, he decided to turn back the way he had come to see if he had gone too far. When he turned around, a big gust of wind pushed him backward. Every time he tried to go north instead of south, another gust of wind made it impossible. Finally, he realized what was happening. Ryla was showing him the way.

South and further south he traveled. On the eighth day, around noon, Buddy looked into the steamy sky as he searched the mountain range. There, just about halfway up the steep incline, he saw something that didn't belong. It was brightly colored. It didn't go up or down; it sort of floated in the air as it lightly swayed from side to side. *What the heck?* thought Buddy. *Could that be Mr. Balloon Billy's place?* He thought it certainly could be. It seemed a good idea to investigate.

It took the rest of the day to find a way leading up to the strange object. Once he found a usable path, he decided to wait until morning before going to the oddity that swung to and fro up in the mountains. Knowing that darker colors absorb the heat from the sun, Buddy found a big black rock to help keep him warm during the night. He curled up into a ball, snuggled close to the rock, and instantly fell fast asleep. That night he had wonderful dreams of the many adventures that lay ahead.

The following morning was especially foggy. Buddy could hardly see the mountain at all. The item of interest was totally blocked by the thick mist. He had found a pathway before he had fallen asleep, and he had marked his bearings like he had promised himself. Being prepared allowed him to forge ahead in spite of the bad weather.

Up the slope he trudged. Sometimes the fog was so thick he could barely see the ground, and sometimes it almost disappeared completely. Each time there was a break in the fog, Buddy searched for the brightly colored thing. Sometimes he found it, and other times it was hidden behind rocks or trees, but he knew it was there.

Early in the afternoon the fog finally lifted. He could now clearly see his destination. He headed straight for it. It was big—very big—and it was floating in the air like a brightly colored upside-down teardrop-shaped cloud that was tied to the ground. This was a curious item indeed. Getting closer, he could see the ropes that held the object. Under the big balloon was a very large pot. The balloon was tied to the pot, and the pot was tied to the ground. Buddy had never seen anything like this before.

Beyond the big pot, Buddy could see a little stone cottage. Behind the dwelling was a large barn with a weather vane pointing out the direction of the wind. There was smoke coming from the cottage chimney, so he called, "Hello in the house, are you there?"

The door to the house burst open. A stubby man with a big belly came out. He had a large, fat handlebar mustache and wore a wide-brimmed, floppy cowboy hat. "What, what; who is there? Do you need a ride?" he sputtered.

"I am Buddy, Buddy Bear from far, far away. I have come from over the mountains. I was told I should see you and that you could help me," Buddy explained.

"Well then, come on in, and we'll talk business," the little man offered.

Buddy went up and entered the sturdy-looking little structure the man called home. "I am Buddy …"

The man interrupted, "I'm not deaf. Nor am I so goofy that I cannot remember what happened just a minute ago. You are a bear looking for help, and you came from far away. Let me introduce myself. I am Billy. Balloon Billy is what they call me because of my balloon out there. It is the only one in the kingdom. I hire myself out to people who need to get somewhere fast. Now, where do you want to go?"

"Um, er, ah," Buddy stammered. "I'm not sure where I want to go. I want to go home, but home is not in the kingdom of Mangonel. Can you take me home?"

"I can only go to places in this kingdom," the man stated with a wrinkled brow. "Sorry, I can't help you."

Buddy asked more questions with the hope of getting some help in at least finding a new destination. "How do you take people to other places? Can you take me? I want to keep heading to the morning sun. Hopefully I will find a way home along the way."

"How do I take people to places?" The little guy raised his eyebrows high as he asked. "Didn't you see the balloon outside? I take anyone to any place they want to go in the kingdom. I float them through the air beneath my giant flying balloon—for a fee, of course."

Buddy was as shocked as the balloon man seemed to be. "So that's a giant flying balloon. How does it work?"

"Never seen a flying balloon before, eh? Well I heat up the air under the balloon out there. The hot air rises up into the balloon. Since the hot air wants to go up, and I have captured the air in my balloon, the balloon goes up, and I ride the wind to wherever I want," Billy explained.

"I have been all the way east to the Silent Sea, as far south as the Great Salt Ocean, and west over the mountains all the way to the Never-Ending Swamp," Billy said with pride. "Never been north though," he added, a bit crestfallen.

Buddy had an idea. "Do you like fish?" he asked.

"I love fish!" exclaimed Balloon Billy.

Buddy inquired if there was a river nearby.

"Just a short distance off to the west," replied Billy.

Buddy formed his plan quickly. "If I go catch you some fish, will you take me in your balloon?"

Billy thought this was a fantastic plan. "That would be a wonderful trade. You've got yourself a deal, Buddy."

"What is the name of the river?" asked the bear.

"River," said Billy.

"Hmmmm! The name of the river is River? Is there any other name for it?"

"Nope," remarked the balloon man, "just River. It's called the River-River. You know, like the sea to the east is called the Silent Sea, the river is called River-River."

Buddy gave up. *Things are surely weird in Mangonel*, he thought. Then he turned, went out the door, faced the west, and trudged on to the River-River to get some fish for the balloon man.

It took several hours, but Buddy finally returned with more fish than Billy had ever seen. Bears are very good at catching fish, but Buddy knew this fishing trip was more luck than skill.

"We will go flying tomorrow," said Billy. "I'm going to cook us a wonderful fish dinner. I think I'll store the rest of these in my snow bank to keep them fresh. We can leave in the morning when we will have more daylight for staying aloft." Then Billy took all the fish and gleefully scampered off into his house to cook his newly acquired treasures.

The meal Billy prepared was truly delicious. After eating, Billy and Buddy sat by the fireplace and talked. Buddy told Billy how he had wished to be a bear while on earth and wound up becoming a bear in Mangonel. He also told stories about the adventures he already had in Mangonel. They were both thankful for the companionship. Buddy and Billy wanted to talk all night long, but tomorrow was going to be an exciting day, and they needed their rest.

Early the next morning, Buddy was shaken awake by his host. The balloon was already tight with hot air, the house had been straightened, and a lunch was packed and ready to go. They went out the door, and the new friends climbed into the big pot. Billy yelled, "Hold on, here we go," as he leaned over the edge of the pot to untie all the lines holding them down.

The balloon sprang upward, giving Buddy a funny feeling in his belly. Up, up, up they went. The ground below looked very different from up in the sky. Buddy couldn't tell where he was or where he had been, even though he had just recently walked over the exact same area. Then he noticed that looking at the ground from up in the air was very much like looking at Ryla's map. Buddy stared out over the vast land and imagined the map on the cave floor. He had a good sense of where everything was now. Off to one side was the desert. It was large and flat. It looked hot even from his vantage point up in the balloon's pot. Running along the edge of the desert were the mountains. Buddy looked for the River-River, but it was hidden by the jagged rocks and tall trees. The mountains stretched to either side of them going north and south. They were majestic, sculptured by God, covered in snow, beautiful to look at, dangerous to climb.

When the balloon rose high enough to catch the wind, Ryla blew them toward the east. Buddy was glad they were heading east, but he had no real destination in mind except to find a way home. He had originally chosen to go east, so continuing in that direction would help him finish searching in that area of Mangonel first. Riding under the big balloon, they would cross the desert high in the air where it was cooler. This was far better than walking across the burning hot sand.

Buddy was first to notice the shift in the wind. Slowly, the balloon turned toward the north, and then more and more westward. Ryla was going to take them over the mountains and into areas even Mr. Balloon Billy had never traveled.

Billy was an adventurer. He cared little of the misdirection they were taking. He just liked going. Buddy was less pleased, but he knew Ryla was going to blow whichever way she wished, and that was all there was to that. Buddy leaned against the edge of the pot to gaze at all the wonderment below. They were on their way to who knew where, maybe home.

Dictionary—Chapter 3

Acquire: *To get possession of something*

Adventurer: *Somebody who enjoys exciting, new activities*

Advice: *An opinion about what another person should do*

Choke: *To gag on something; to blurt out a remark in short, harsh tones*

Committed: *Devoted to somebody*

Companionship: *The company of friends*

Continue: *To keep going*

Curious: *Eager to know about something or to get information*

Crestfallen: *Disappointed, especially after being enthusiastic or confident*

Deaf: *Partially or completely unable to hear*

Delicious: *Having an enjoyable taste*

Descend: *To go down a staircase, hill, or other incline*

Destination: *The place to which somebody or something is going or must go*

Especially: *Unusual, exceptional*

Exchanged: *To give something and receive something in return*

Express: *To say something; to convey a meaning*

Fantastic: *Much larger than usual or expected; also something that is extraordinarily good*

Forge: *To move slowly and steadily*

Impossible: *Not able to exist or to be done*

Interrupt: *To stop someone from speaking by talking over him or her*

Introduce: *To make yourself or another person known to somebody else*

Knowledge: *Clear awareness of information*

Lethargy: *Tiredness, lack of energy*

Majestic: *Greatly impressive in appearance*

Misdirection: *The wrong direction*

Protection: *Something that prevents someone or something from being damaged*

Realize: *To know, understand, and accept*

Scamper: *A quick and playful run*

Sculpture: *A three-dimensional work of art. A statue*

Shock: *An unexpected experience that has a sudden effect on somebody*

Sputter: *To pronounce words in a popping, explosive way, especially when angry or excited*

Stammer: *To speak or say something with many quick hesitations and repeated consonants or syllables*

Stubby: *Short, thick, broad, or blunt*

Trudge: *To walk with slow, weary steps*

Wonderment: *Surprised and admiring something*

CHAPTER 4

The Land of Helpers

Buddy Bear and his new friend, Balloon Billy, had left Billy's cabin in the mountains in a hot air balloon. They were hoping to head east on Buddy's quest to find his way out of the kingdom of Mangonel and back home to his mother in the Colorado Rocky Mountains. Apparently Ryla of the Wind had different plans. Shortly after they left the ground, the balloon caught a gust of wind that raised them high into the air. A perfect breeze began blowing them eastward; then it shifted. It started blowing them back toward the northwest, right where they had come from.

The large pot under the balloon gently rocked as it was carried along by the quiet, peaceful breeze. Ryla guided them straight through a pass in the mountains. They crossed over the River-River. Even though they couldn't see them, Buddy was sure the trails he walked on, and the river he fished in, were directly below their flight path. He recognized some sections of the mountain trails that periodically peeked through the foliage below the balloon. Buddy and Balloon Billy passed over an evergreen forest, and then the wind changed again, driving them farther north and west. They sailed over the strangest building either of them had ever seen. It was a castle, but from their point of view in the balloon, it looked like it was right-side up. If that was the case, then the building would have to be upside down on the ground! The kingdom of Mangonel really was full of odd things. They floated over the castle unnoticed by those below. On and on they went.

Several hours earlier, the two travelers enjoyed a fish sandwich while they continued to watch the ground slowly slip by. Buddy was getting hungry again, and the sun was setting in the western sky. The day was drawing to an end. Billy started releasing some of the hot air from inside the balloon in order for them to land for the night. With each puff of air released, they slowly dropped farther from the sky. Billy did this several times until the pot they were riding in bumped the ground. A final bit of air was released, and the pot settled gently in a large, grassy meadow.

While they were up in the sky, Buddy had noticed a town to the north. He told Billy he wanted to go there to see if he could find them something to eat. Billy agreed that Buddy should go, but he was going to stay with his balloon. Then he warned Buddy, "Be back before dawn. Otherwise my balloon and I will go on without you." Buddy understood. With this arrangement in place the bear cub turned north and began walking toward the town.

After floating in the sky, it felt strange walking on the ground. It was like jumping on a trampoline, then jumping on concrete. It's was very strange sensation when the ground suddenly didn't flex.

It was nice that the town was not far away. When Buddy crossed over the first hill he was able to see it clearly.

In just a short time, Buddy was walking into the town on a hard-packed dirt street. It was a quiet place. With the exception of some children playing, everyone seemed to be inside. The smell of many different meals filled the air. It was suppertime, and the various aromas made Buddy salivate. As he approached the playing children, they didn't seem to be alarmed in the slightest. They had never seen a bear, and so they had no reference to warn them there might be danger in this large animal. When he was close to the little group of children, he told them he was a hungry traveler looking for some food. They all started shouting how they could take him home for dinner.

"I can help, I can help," they screamed with delight.

Boy, what a friendly town this is, thought Buddy.

Buddy held his paws up for silence. "I will choose with whom I will go," he called. He then began to count around the group with "eeny, meeny, miny, mo." He couldn't remember all the words to the little poem so he said, "I'll choose the child with whom I'll go. Eeny, meeny, miny, mo." He stopped counting while he was pointing to a little, dark-haired girl. "You," he said, "I will go with you."

The little girl ran up, grabbed his paw, and began pulling him along the street, exclaiming, "Yay, I'm helping!" She took Buddy up to the front door of a nice little house with a bright red door. It looked warm and cozy.

"Come on in," said the girl.

Buddy could barely fit through the door. It was then he realized he was growing and growing very fast. He had had nothing familiar to reference his size, so he just thought he was the same, but this wasn't so. In the few weeks he had been in Mangonel he had more than doubled his size. Buddy was a grizzly bear, and they grow really big. He was not going to be a runt by any means. By the time he was finished growing, he would be nearly ten feet tall when he stood on his hind legs. He would weigh over eight hundred pounds and be very strong. He was going to be one of the largest beings in Mangonel when he was fully grown.

Inside the house, to the left of the front door entrance, was the living room. Soft chairs were set along two of the four walls in that room. To the right was a large table with ten chairs. A place setting rested in front of every chair. They were ready for dinner. Just past the dining table was the kitchen, where a skinny lady, wrapped in a stained apron was cooking in great big pots and pans. She turned to see who had come into her house. She nearly screamed when she saw the big bear standing next to her daughter. Since the bear was not acting in any aggressive manner, she asked, "Leelo, what have you there?"

Leelo, felt a little embarrassed, "I'm sorry, I don't know his name, but he is hungry. Guess what? Out of all the other kids, he chose me to help." Leelo was very proud of being chosen.

Buddy stumbled over his words at first, but eventually he was able to explain who he was and how Balloon Billy flew him to a place just outside of town. All this was extremely strange to the people in the house. They had never seen or heard of Balloon Billy. Not a single person had ever traveled outside of the town, but they seemed very willing to help Buddy in any way they could. All at once, Leelo and her two sisters, five brothers, and father were all pushing and shoving to be the first to get a chair for Buddy. Without a chance to say a word, he found himself seated at the head of the dining table.

The mother followed behind the rest with a large bowl of the porridge she had been preparing and an equally large spoon. The entire family had gathered so close around Buddy he couldn't lift his arms to feed himself. Then everything went crazy. The whole family started yelling about how Buddy obviously needed help with this, or help with that, and they pushed in closer. One had a napkin, one grabbed the spoon from the table and started shoveling food into Buddy's mouth. At the same time, another had some bread he was trying to stuff into the bear's mouth. The one with the napkin kept wiping at Buddy's face, while another kept pushing his chair in closer to the table. Two boys took turns pouring water all over his face in an effort to get some into his mouth, but the bread, or spoon, or napkin were always in the way. Every time a spoonful of porridge went into Buddy's mouth, the mother refilled the bowl. They were crowding him something awful, and Buddy was getting uncomfortable.

Finally, he had had enough. He sprang from the chair and twirled in a circle to get the people to back away from him. "What is wrong with you?" he roared. There was no answer from anyone, but they began to come close again. They started shouting things like, "He needs a bath." "I'll run the water." "I want to get the soap." "Maybe he is cold, I will get a blanket." "No, no, can't you see he is hot? I'll open the windows." They were all being so helpful they were becoming a nuisance.

Buddy had to twirl around again to get them away once more without hurting them. Shaking his head from side to side, he shouted, "Stop. Can't you see I'm just fine? All I wanted was something to eat. You are doing too much. Please, let me feed myself."

The father took a step forward. Everyone else stood there with their mouths wide open in surprise and shock. The disappointed father looked into Buddy's eyes. "You are in the Land of the Helpers. Everyone here tries very hard to help everyone else. We have helped each other for so long, there is little we can do for each other. You are new to the town. All we want to do is help you. It is what we do. Now, sit down and we'll help you get some more food." Once again, they all started moving closer to Buddy.

These people wanted to help too much. Helping is a good thing, but if you get carried away, you can become more of a problem than a help. Buddy was already full. He felt it best to get out while he was still standing. "I thank you for the food you have given me, but I really must be on my way," Buddy announced as he forced his way to the door. The house was full of chatter about how they could help open the door, walk him out of town, or show him the way to go to keep him safe. The suggestions went on and on. While they were all trying to decide how best help their guest, Buddy snuck out the door, and ran to the edge of town, thinking he might never ask for help again.

Outside the town limits, it was dark. There was no moon, and the stars didn't give off much light. Buddy searched the field for Billy and his balloon but couldn't find him anywhere. He called and called, but there was no answer. In time, he decided to get some sleep. He would get up early to search for Mr. Billy in the morning when he could see more clearly.

The sun shining on Buddy's face brought him rudely awake. He jumped up and quickly searched the field. There was no sign of Billy or his balloon. When he looked back in the direction of the town, he saw the balloon slowly rising in the air on the opposite side of where the Helpers live. Buddy had gotten sidetracked in the dark. Now Balloon Billy was going on his way without him.

A few minutes passed, and the balloon passed right over Buddy's head. Buddy shouted up to the balloonist, but Billy was too high up to hear him calling. Buddy, the grizzly bear, was alone once again. He wanted to go back south and east. He was not looking forward to crossing the mountains again, but there was no getting around it. He needed to finish his search for home in that area of Mangonel. It was something that just had to be done. The town with all the helpers was right in his path. He was determined not to go there again. Buddy stood in the open field staring at the town, and asked himself, "What to do, what to do?"

Dictionary—Chapter 4

Apparently: *What seems to be*

Approach: *Come closer to*

Chatter: *Talking rapidly about unimportant things*

Disappointed: *Not happy because something did not happen the way it was hoped*

Embarrassed: *Ill at ease, ashamed, or humiliated*

Eventually: *After a long time*

Evergreen: *Plants that do not have leaves that stay green all year long*

Exclaim: *To speak or cry out loudly and suddenly*

Extremely: *To a very high degree*

Foliage: *The leaves of a plant or tree*

Gliding: *The act of flying or to move along so smoothly it appears to be flying*

Meadow: *An area of low-lying grassland, especially near a river*

Nuisance: *Annoying or irritating*

Obviously: *Used to suggest that there can be no doubt or uncertainty about something*

Opposite: *The reverse of something*

Periodically: *Once in a while*

Porridge: *Oatmeal*

Quest: *A search for something*

Recognize: *To identify a thing or a person*

Reference: *Comment on something or somebody intending to bring something to mind*

Rudely: *Offensive, to do something in a way that is not polite*

Runt: *An animal considered to be smaller than normal*

Salivate: *To produce saliva in the mouth, especially at an increased rate*

Sidetracked: *Gone off course, headed in an unintended direction*

Suggestions: *Ideas*

Uncomfortable: *Not feeling comfortable, feeling awkward or ill at ease*

Unnoticed: *Went unseen*

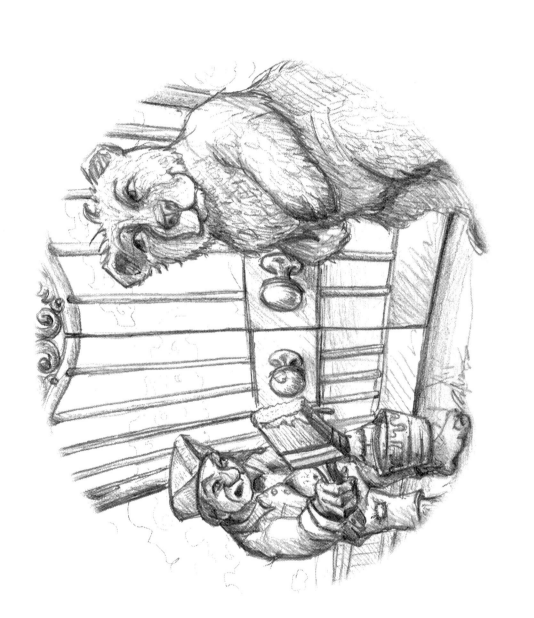

CHAPTER 5

The Gateways of Mangonel

After being assisted by the people in the Land of the Helpers, which was not a pleasant experience, Buddy didn't want to go back through that town again. When he had left the night before, it was dark, and he left in a hurry. The next morning he found himself on the wrong side of the town as he watched his friend Balloon Billy sail by high in the sky. It was just as well. Billy was headed farther into northwest, and Buddy was determined to get back to the east. To avoid being helped again, Buddy headed southeast a good distance away from the perimeter of the town. Eventually he arrived at the spot where Balloon Billy had landed the big pot and had waited for Buddy's return. Putting the town to his back, and positioning himself so the sun was shining over his left shoulder, Buddy faced toward the southeast, exactly where he wanted to go. Taking this direction, he should wind up back near the Wishing Forest. When he got there, maybe he could find a tree that would grant him a wish that would place him east of the desert. That would certainly save a lot of walking.

It was getting late in the morning when Buddy spotted a little fence with a large gate. It was easy to see, even though it was in the distance. The large plain of rolling green grass made the yellow fence stand out like a beacon from a lighthouse. Going to it would take Buddy off his course but only a short distance. He decided to head toward the gate and fence. Soon he arrived at his destination. There was nothing else around, just this little fence with a very tall gate. Why was it here in the middle of nowhere?

The entire fence was only thirty feet in length and just two feet high. However, the gate was about twelve feet high, and it took up ten feet of the thirty-foot fence. Buddy inspected the barrier and then the gate. He walked around the structure to inspect it from the opposite side. Since the fence was only up to his knees, he stepped over it to inspect the first side again. This tiny fence stopped no one, and the gate seemed to serve no purpose. The gate and fence were painted the brightest yellow you ever did see. If you think of the nicest, brightest sunflower you can remember, you have a pretty good idea of how yellow the fence and gate were. The paint was clean and fresh. Some parts even looked like the paint was still wet.

Buddy decided to open the large gate so he could go through it. After all, someone had gone through a great deal of trouble to build it, and it looked like someone was still taking care of it, so it must be there for a reason. The gate had to be built for something, but what? Buddy reached for the knob, but before he could touch it, the knob turned on its own. Then the gate began to open. When it had swung fully open, a tiny man came through carrying a pail of yellow paint, a brush, and a ladder. He wore no shoes, and his bare feet stuck out from under his pants, which were far too short. The pant legs stopped just above his ankles. His undersized trousers were held in place at his waist with a length of rope. The man's shirt was too small as well. The top two buttons were fastened, but the remaining buttons were left undone, making room for his round belly to stick out. The man's clothing, face, hands, and even his feet were covered with blotches of spilled yellow paint. He was mumbling to himself, not paying much attention, so he walked right into Buddy's belly.

"Ooooph," Buddy said, puffing.

With wide eyes, the fellow started yelling in a thick accent. It could have been Scottish, Irish, or a mix of both. "Who air you? What 'ave ye done?" he demanded. "'Ave ye messed up me paint again? So you air the one who's been a toochin' me wet paint all these yars. I keep paintin' an' you keep toochin'. Let me see yer 'ands. There 'as to be yellow paint on 'em, doesn't there! Why do you keep messin' up me paint?" As the little man rambled on, Buddy walked around the fence and gate again. There was nothing. Where did this guy come from?

As Buddy gently pushed the man to the side and stuck his head through the opening, he told the tiny painter his name, where he was from, and where he was trying to go. *Amazing,* thought Buddy. The south side of the gate was entirely different from the north side. Buddy poked his head through the gate several times, and then he went all the way through and back again. *How very strange,* he thought.

"Who are you?" asked Buddy. "Can you explain this gate?"

"If it will keep yer paws off the paint, I'll explain it to ye. No offense about the paws remark."

The man put a lid on his bucket, placed it on the ground, and sat upon it. "Me name is Patrick Michael McDougal Oshay. I passed through a gate much like this one a long time agoo, and I've noot bin home since. I searched this place oop and down. No matter how hard I searched, I found no way to return home. Me searchin' took me far an' wide in this strange place, but I found noo other gate but this one. It looks so like the one that broot me here, don't ya know! It were in terrible repair, so I decided to fix it. I had noo tools ta work wit, but one day a peddler in a wee wagon passed by, an' he sold me tools, bruushes, and paint. I keeps the fence and gate in good shape, 'cause I'm thinkin', someday I will pass through, and it will take me home again.

"Me job is never endin'. Someone keeps toochin me wet paint as soon as I'm finished. Watch, I'll show ye." The man grabbed a brush full of paint and quickly touched up the handle. He picked up his pail, told Buddy to follow him, and in order to open the gate, promptly took hold of the handle he had just finished painting. Once on the other side, he closed the gate, and then pointed to the messy handle on that side. "See thar, I just finished toochin' that up before I ran inta you." Then, Patrick Michael McDougal Oshay painted the messy latch. He immediately grabbed it so they could go back to the grassy plain side. When they were back on the north side of the fence, Patrick Michael McDougal Oshay turned and pointed at the messed-up handle. "See? Can't ye see how someone keeps sneakin' aboot toochin' me paint? I canna catch 'im. He's too fast."

Buddy saw what was going on. He tried to explain to Mr. Oshay that it was he, himself who was touching the paint. It took some explaining because Patrick Michael refused to believe he was messing things up all this time, but eventually he said he understood, though he really didn't.

Then Buddy asked, "Why does everything change when you pass through the gate?"

Patrick Michael looked at Buddy as if he had come from the moon. He gave this explanation: "Ya see, it's like this, laddie. When ye pass through a door ta go inside, the inside is noot like the outside, tis it? An' when ye go through a door from the inside to the outside, it ain't like bein' inside anymore. That is the way it is with these gates.

"Now, I been told there air many a gate in Mangonel, and some tis like this one thet takes ya from one place in Mangonel to another place in Mangonel withoot all the walkin', an' then thar am them others thet will take ya ta someplace altogether different, maybe back home on earth where ye came from, or it could take ya just aboot anywhar."

Here was a bit of good news! Buddy might not have to walk all over Mangonel, step by step. If he could find more of these passages, maybe he would find a gate back to Colorado.

Patrick Michael McDougal Oshay went back to painting one side of the gate, and then the next. Buddy knew he had not understood that he was messing things up on his own, so he asked Mr. Oshay to open the gate for him so as not to disturb the freshly painted handle. Buddy went through the open space and into a new area of Mangonel. As he began to walk away, he could hear Patrick Michael mumbling about the mystery man who could sneak in so fast, ruin his paint, and disappear.

On the south side of the fence, off to Buddy's left, there stood a forest. Going to it, he eventually could hear the gurgling of a stream as it rushed over some rocks. The stream was hidden by a thick group of trees that lined the beautiful forest. Some of the trees in this part of Mangonel were unlike any trees Buddy had ever seen. The leaves were big and broad. Some of the branches and leaves were covered in a stringy moss and vines. The leaves themselves came in a wide variety of colors. Some were purple, some were orange, and others were brown; still more were blue, green, or yellow. They were strange, even for Mangonel. "I wonder where I am now," Buddy commented to himself.

It was time to get something to eat, so Buddy headed toward the sound of the water. There might be fish in that stream. When he reached the little creek that ran through the trees, he saw a bridge and went over to it. He then stooped down to take a drink of the cold, clear water. When he stood up, there was the ugliest, biggest, and meanest-looking being he had ever seen.

Dictionary—Chapter 5

Amazing: *Outstanding, wonderful, barely believable*

Beacon: *A beam of light, like from a flashing light*

Certainly: *Without doubt*

Comment: *To say something that states a fact or expresses an opinion*

Determined: *Feeling or showing firmness or a fixed purpose*

Experience: *Active involvement in an activity or exposure to events or people over a period of time that leads to an increase in knowledge or skill*

Gurgling: *To say something with a bubbling sound in the throat*

Inspect: *To look at something carefully*

Lighthouse: *A building, often tall, with a powerful flashing light on the top to guide ships at sea from the dangerous shore*

Mumbling: *To say something quietly and not clearly*

Offense: *An attack as in an insult*

Positioning: *Placing something in a specific spot*

Promptly: *Right away*

Refuse: *Declare to not do something*

CHAPTER 6

Buddy and the Fable Forest

Buddy had just passed through a gate that warped distances, or something like that. He had stumbled upon the large gate by accident while trying to get away from the Land of the Helpers. When he passed through the big opening, he found one side of the gate was completely different from the other. On the north side there was a large grassland, and on the south side there was a forest. The man who took care of the passageway, Mr. Patrick Michael McDougal Oshay, had a funny accent, and he told Buddy there were more gates and passages within Mangonel that could take him from one place to another. Some might even transfer him back to earth.

As Buddy took a drink of water from a sparkling stream, he paid little attention to the shadow that had passed over him. When he was about to stand up, there before him was the biggest creature he had ever seen. By this time, Buddy was getting to be a pretty big bear, but he was still short compared to the thing staring down at him.

A little scared, Buddy squeaked a greeting. "Hello, I am Buddy, a bear from Colorado, on earth. I got trapped here in Mangonel, and I am trying to find my way home. Who ..." Buddy was halted by the look on the creature's face.

The monster just looked at Buddy. Then he raised an enormous club. Holding it in both hands, he slowly rested it across the front of his stomach.

Buddy quickly went on. "Hey, wait just a minute. I'm just passing through. There is no reason to get angry." Then, while he still had a smidgen of control of the situation, he asked in a friendly way, "Is this your stream? Do you live here? What is your name, friend?"

The creature finally said something. In a menacing voice, he demanded, "Are ya gonna cross dis he-a stream or not?"

"I'm really not sure at the moment. Perhaps I will later on," answered Buddy.

"Good, ya hasta go up ta da bridge an cross dare. Dats where I lives, and dat bridge belong ta me. You gonna hasta pay me a toll, or you no gonna go cross my bridge," ordered the creature. Obviously, this thing was not very friendly or very bright.

Buddy, knowing now that the monster was a bit dimwitted, took pity on him. He also capitalized on the moment of silence to continue his inquiry. "Who are you? What's your name? Why do I need to cross your bridge when I can just walk across this tiny stream right here?"

The creature filled his chest with pride as he pointed his large club toward the bridge. "I em a troll, and I em da onliest troll in alla Mangonel. Evabody jus calls me Troll. Ain't got no udder name. I builded dat bridge, and ennyone who crosses dis stream on my bridge pays me a toll. An evabody crosses on my bridge cause iffen day don, den I bonks 'em with my club. Now you gonna pay, or em I gonna hasta bonk ya?" Troll got an odd look on his face. It was clear he was thinking very hard about something. After a span of silence, he began again. "I almos' forgot sumpin'. After I bonks ya, om supposed ta eat ya."

Buddy couldn't believe what he was hearing. "Why in the world would you do such a thing?"

"Dis is hows it goes. Ain't ya never heard of da *Three Billy Goats Gruff*?" asked Troll. When Buddy said he had not, Troll went on with his story. "Well, iffen yer goona do dis right, yer suppose ta try an fool me, an tell me ya gots a bigger brother comin' fer me ta eat, an so I should lets ya go." He put a dirty finger in his mouth while he waited. Removing the finger so he could speak, he said, "So, watcha waitin fer? Gets on wid it."

The creature waited some more, and then Buddy, not accustomed to telling lies, came back with, "I have no brother coming down this path, and neither do I have anything with which to pay you. What do we do now? What happened next in the story?"

Confused, Troll tried to sort the mess out. Holding the club in one hand, he scratched his head. Then he shifted the club and dug a finger of the other hand into his ear. "Well, wit no brothers an' no money, I ain't sure what ta do next. You bigger brother is suppose' to say he has even a bigger brother comin'. Then I lets him go, and the biggest brother comes an' I get scared or somethin', cause he is so big, an' I lets him go too. Now you gots nobody comin', an' ya gots no money; whatdaya think we should do? You is a nice fella; I hates to bonk ya."

Buddy contemplated his next move. "Since you wind up letting everyone go across the bridge in the end, why don't we just skip the parts about the other brothers, and just let me go over the bridge?"

"Heck no, caint do dat," said Troll.

"Why not?"

"Cause you don't scare me or nuttin'," argued Troll.

Buddy was trying to think about what he should do, when along came a fox. Her voice was soft, yet her accent made it seem like she came from royalty, though she hadn't. "I say, what goes on here?" asked the fox in a distinctively British accent. Buddy and Troll both tried to explain at the same time.

"Just one moment," stated the fox. "I do believe I understand your problem. This reminds me of one of the many stories I used to listen to from outside a child's window while I rummaged through some of their … um … er … refuse. The mother would recite from a book she called *Aesop's Fables*. You, Mr. Troll, if I am not mistaken, are from one of those fables, are you not? And you, bear, like me, are from earth. Mr. Troll is reliving the fable of the *Three Billy Goats Gruff* and wants a fee paid, that you, Mr. Bear, have no means for paying. To settle the problem, neither of you desire to bonk or be bonked." After some meditation, the fox spoke again. "A solution comes to mind." The fox turned to face Troll. "Don't you wish others to cross your lovely bridge and admire your handiwork?" Troll nodded yes. "And don't you like it when someone praises your fine work?" Another nod was the only answer from the ugly troll. "So, if we were to cross your bridge and tell you how wonderfully strong and beautiful it is, wouldn't that be enough payment?" Troll looked confused, but since the fox seemed to be very smart, the slow-witted creature figured she knew best, so he agreed.

All three walked over to the bridge. Buddy and the fox passed over the stream on the rickety bridge the troll had built, all the while exclaiming in very loud voices how nice the bridge was and how much they enjoyed crossing the stream on Troll's magnificent bridge. Troll was very pleased indeed.

When Buddy and the fox were on the other side, the shrewd fox turned to Troll once more. "Now, Mr. Troll, if you wish to be paid by those crossing your bridge, I suggest you lend us some coins and perhaps a bag to carry them in. Since we have nothing to satisfy your fee on this occasion, it is likely we will not have the funds when we next meet. We wouldn't want to be faced with this same situation upon our return, would we?"

"Um! No. S'pose not. You gots a good idea dare, fox," said Troll as he went below the bridge to gather a sack and some of his money to lend to Buddy and the fox. Now they would have something to pay the troll the next time they tried to use his bridge. The troll handed the sack to Buddy because it was nearly full of gold, silver, and copper coins. At least he knew enough not to give the sack to the tiny fox. It was far too heavy for her to carry.

"Thank you ever so much. Please pay the troll, Mr. Bear, and we will be off," said the fox. As soon as a few coins had been handed back to the smiling troll, the clever fox began pulling Buddy down the little pathway, away from the troll and his bridge. "We most certainly do not wish to be present should the creature discover our ruse," suggested the fox in a hushed voice.

"You are a sly one, Miss Fox," said Buddy without moving his lips. "What is your name, and where are you headed?"

The fox perked up when she heard the term *sly*. "No matter my name. Today I choose a new one. From this day forward, I will be known as Silvia Fox and be addressed with a shortened version, Sly."

While walking, the two shared their stories. Sly the Fox explained how she had come from England. She told Buddy about how she had fallen into a stream that carried her to a waterfall. At the bottom of the falls, she was sucked downward until she was pushed into the air by a geyser at the head of the troll's stream. Buddy told Sly all the things he knew of Mangonel. Sly listened with great interest.

"If it is acceptable to you, I should think it prudent that we travel together. Oh, sorry, prudent means good sense," said the fox. She continued, "Let me offer this. I wish to be your traveling companion. With your brawn and my intelligence, we could be of great service to one another. I mean, we could help each other. What say you?"

Buddy couldn't have been more pleased. Finally, he had someone to travel with. Maybe they could help each other find their way back to earth.

The new friends spent days wandering through the Fable Forest. They came across many of their favorite fable characters. They stayed long enough with each new character to listen to their entire story again and again and again. It was much more interesting hearing the tales from the actual participants.

During their visits with characters from *The Tortoise and the Hare, The Little Dog and His Bone, The Fox and the Grapes,* and *The Lion and the Mouse,* they found out how these storybook creatures came to life. The legend in Mangonel was that a copy of *Aesop's Fables* fell into a river, and at the bottom of a large waterfall, it was pushed down through the earth and up into a geyser at the beginning of the River of Life. This sounded very familiar to Sly's experience. When the book entered the water that Troll calls his own, the characters all came out of the book and became living creatures. The stream was their source of life. All of the living creatures from the fables must go to the River of Life to drink every day or they will dry up and become paper again, so they never stray far from the stream of life-giving water.

The Fable Forest and all the characters who lived there were great fun, but Buddy and Sly were growing tired of the same stories being told over and over. So, one day, while all the characters were away getting their daily drink from the river, they chose a southeasterly direction—Buddy's idea—and began to march directly through the center of the forest and out the other side. Buddy had never been in this area of Mangonel before. All the forthcoming adventures were going to be new for both Buddy Bear and Silvia Fox.

Dictionary—Chapter 6

Accent: *A certain and distinctive way of pronouncing something*

Acceptable: *Considered to be satisfactory*

Accustomed: *Something that you are familiar with and have come to expect*

Admire: *To regard somebody with approval, appreciation, or respect*

Aesop's Fables: *A collection of short stories, each with a moral*

Brawn: *Very strong muscles, especially on the arms and legs*

Capitalize: *To profit or take advantage of something*

Characters: *One of the people or animals mentioned in a book*

Clever: *Sharp mental abilities*

Companion: *Somebody who accompanies or shares time with another*

Completely: *The full extent of something*

Confused: *Unable to think clearly, unsure*

Contemplated: *Thought about something*

Dimwitted: *Not very smart*

Distinctively: *Unique*

Enormous: *Very large*

Fable: *A short story with a moral, especially one in which the characters are animals*

Forthcoming: *Something that will happen in the near future*

Geyser: *A spring that throws a jet of water or steam into the air at intervals*

Inquire: *To ask a question*

Intelligence: *The ability to learn facts and skills and then apply them*

Magnificent: *Beautiful and impressive*

Meditate: *To concentrate on one thought*

Menacing: *Threatening*

Praises: *Words that express admiration*

Refuse: *Garbage*

Rummage: *To make a careless and rapid search*

Satisfy: *To fulfill a need or desire*

Situation: *The current conditions that characterize somebody's life or events in a particular place*

Stray: *To wander off*

Solution: *The answer to a problem*

Version: *A form or variety of something that is different from others or the original form*

Warped: *To become twisted or out of shape or make something become twisted or out of shape*

CHAPTER 7

Dangerous Desert

Leaving the Fable Forest and the giant troll behind, Buddy Bear and Sly Fox marched through the forest and entered a large flat plain. The grass was short, red as a ripe tomato, and difficult to see because of the fog that covered the land. The farther they went onto the plain, the foggier it became. In very little time they lost all sense of direction. The fog was all around them. There was no escaping it. The air was much cooler here, and there was a constant breeze coming from one direction. Having no way to determine which way they were going, Sly Fox, with her brilliant mind, told Buddy that it stood to reason that if the breeze was blowing in one direction, and the fog can be blown away, then it would be best to head into the wind to see if they could walk out of the fog.

It took days to find their way clear of the annoying, dense fog. They eventually broke free, but the icy breeze that was chilling their bones was worse than ever. Now that they could see, they noticed the wind was coming down from the snowcapped mountains and across a frozen plateau. Sly explained to Buddy that this was why there was so much fog. The cold, damp air was meeting the warmer air of the plains. This condition is what was causing the condensation or fog. If Sly was correct, and she seemed to be correct most of the time, the plain they were on might never be clear of fog. If Buddy and Sly were ever going to go east in clearer weather, they would have to continue south to travel around the fog.

Ryla had told Buddy that the mountains went north and south, so he and Sly figured if they followed the mountains south, they would be going away from the Fable Forest and away from the fog. When they traveled far enough to the south, they could turn east again. So off they went, heading south.

Every hour it got warmer and warmer. At one point, Buddy looked back and saw there was no sign of the fog. Sly also noticed the mist was no longer in sight. They agreed it was time to turn east. The very next day they began going toward the sun once more. Not long into their easterly journey, they found themselves in sand—lots and lots of sand. Buddy remembered the map Ryla had drawn. With all this barren land, he knew they were in the desert. Ryla had warned him of this place and how very dangerous it could be, but Sly paid no attention. She insisted they continue pushing east.

By the third day, the two friends were awfully thirsty, and still there was nothing but sand. They sat down behind a small dune to get out of the afternoon sun. Sly began to dig in the hot sand. She was trying to find some cooler dirt to rest in. Buddy needed someplace cool to rest too, so he dug a hole as well. Buddy was much bigger than Sly, so his hole was much deeper. The deeper he dug, the cooler it got. Buddy wanted the coolest dirt he could find, so he kept on digging. Sly was fast asleep in her little hole before Buddy finished making a hole big enough for him to rest in.

In time, the sand in Buddy's hole became slightly moist, so he dug a bit more. Then he curled up in his own cool space for a short rest. He fell asleep almost instantly. A few hours passed. Suddenly he was awakened because he couldn't breathe. He sat up choking and coughing. In his sleep, he had inhaled some of the water he was resting in.

The water had come up slowly from the ground where Buddy had dug his hole. "Sly, come quickly," he yelled. The fox poked her head over the lip of Buddy's pit. It was difficult to describe how overjoyed she was to see the water. They both drank small amounts at first to keep from getting sick, and then they drank until they had their fill. It was very refreshing.

Back on the march, they went deeper and deeper into the Dangerous Desert. Whenever they found themselves in a shaded area, Buddy would dig a deep hole and wait. Sometimes water would seep into the bottom of the hole; sometimes it would not. There were no berries, no grasses, no trees, nothing to eat, and nothing to drink. If they didn't find their way across this wasteland soon, they would surely die.

One morning Buddy awoke to find Sly missing. He was terribly worried. Did something come in the night and run off with Sly to eat her? Did Sly think she was a burden to Buddy and leave so he would have a better chance alone? Did she become delirious, and not knowing what she was doing, wander off? Buddy sat by the rock they had chosen, put his head between his knees, and began to cry. Even big people cry when they are very sad, and Buddy thought he had never been so sad. His new friend and traveling companion was gone.

"Why are you weeping?" cooed a familiar voice.

Buddy looked up. There, in the hot desert sun, stood Sly the Fox. She was all smiles, and so was Buddy. "I thought you had wandered off. I thought maybe something bad had happened. I was afraid I would never see you again. Don't ever do that again," he said as he hugged her so tight she gasped for air.

Sly pushed Buddy back. "I'm sorry I startled you. I promise I will let you know where I'm going next time," she promised. "Oh, but you just must forgive me. I have been foraging. That is to say, I went about in an attempt to find some food. If you will follow me, I have a surprise for you."

Buddy got up and followed Sly deeper into the desert. All the while, the fox kept telling him that sooner or later they would reach the center of the desert. When they got that far into the wasteland, they would be able to begin their march out. Buddy didn't understand why they needed to go all the way into the desert first. Why didn't they start their way out right now?

Sly explained, "You see, old boy, once we have gotten to the center, any direction will lead us out. Imagine you are in the middle of a circle; every direction is the same distance to the edge. At that location, no direction will lead you back in. When we reach the midpoint, we will be halfway through this dreaded place." Buddy got the idea, and it cheered him up.

Sly was in the lead, but it seemed she was going in circles, looking for something. "Blast this land; I can't find my tracks on the hard-packed sections of ground, and the wind has blown sand over my tracks where the soil is soft. I do believe we should separate while we search. We mustn't lose sight of each other. Keep a close watch. Look for a mound of mud about four feet high. It looks like an upside-down cone."

As they searched, they entered an area where there were some stubby plants. All of them had long spikes, no leaves, and dried bark. They looked dead. There were no fruit or berries on any of them. Buddy shook his head as he continued searching for the mound of dirt Sly had mentioned. Many minutes later he heard the fox call out, "Yahoo! Come this way, chap; this way!" Buddy raced over to Sly, but he couldn't see anything that would make the fox so happy.

"Here, here, my friend. This mound is a termite mound. It is full of juicy, nutritious termites. They don't taste very good, but they are full of protein, and their fat little bodies have the moisture we need to survive. Now, forget about how they taste, and eat."

Buddy did as the fox commanded. Sly was right. They tasted horrible, and they squirmed around in his paws and in his mouth. Yuck! After he had eaten a few paws full of the termites, he got used to it. He began to eat them by the bunch. He felt like he was hungry enough to eat almost anything, and the termite meal was just the thing to fill his belly. Eating the termites proved one thing: he truly could eat almost anything. It struck Buddy funny how a full stomach can make you ready to conquer the world, even the Dangerous Desert.

When they finished eating, Buddy moved to the shady side of the termite mound, leaned back against the little hill, and closed his eyes. It was a great time to relax. Opening his eyes, he saw a little dark cloud in the sky. No, it wasn't a cloud, it was smoke. He got up and climbed to the top of the termite dune to see the smoke more clearly. It was coming from behind a butte. How did he know it was a butte? Ryla must have mentioned it. It came to him in his head: *a butte is a hill or small mountain that rises sharply from the ground*. He had never seen a butte before, but somehow he knew what it was. "Come look," Buddy called to Sly.

The two stared at the smoke. Then, when it registered in their minds what they were looking at, they both jumped up and down with joy. If they had any luck at all, the fire would mean there was someone close by who started it. If there was someone there, they might be able to get some information. Perhaps there would be food and shelter available too. Buddy and Sly turned to face each other, gave out a yell, and started down the little hill they were standing on. They walked briskly toward the smoke and hopefully toward someone who could help them.

The distance was much greater than it appeared from the dune. It took two days to reach the bottom of the huge buttes. As they got closer, they discovered there wasn't just one butte but a cluster of them. At the bottom of the huge natural structures, the smoke had disappeared. The rocky cliffs of the buttes were exceptionally large. Sly said it would probably take another day to go around them, but it was cooler near these jutting hills, and for that, they were thankful.

In the sparse shade provided by the rocks, the two friends realized they had used nearly all of their energy trying to reach the place where the smoke was coming from. Being so tired is not the time to venture into a new and unknown circumstance. They picked the safer choice by deciding to get plenty of rest before starting out again in the morning. They needed to know what caused the smoke, and they hoped that when they got there, they would find someone friendly. Only time would tell. Tomorrow would answer all their questions.

Dictionary—Chapter 7

Annoying: *Causing mild anger or impatience*

Brilliant: *Exceptional, extraordinary ability, talent, or intelligence*

Burden: *A difficult or worrisome responsibility*

Butte: *A hill that rises abruptly from a flat area of land, with steep sides and a flat top.*

Consideration: *Careful thought*

Constant: *Always present*

Conquer: *To master something*

Coo: *To speak with exaggerated admiration or sympathy*

Delirious: *Confused and unable to make wise choices or decisions*

Exceptional: *Above average*

Forage: *A search or the process of searching for something, especially a search for food and supplies*

Instantly: *Without delay*

Nutritious: *Containing minerals and vitamins that promote health*

Overjoyed: *Very pleased, more than just happy*

Plateau: *An area of high ground with a fairly level surface on top*

Refreshing: *Serving to bring back energy*

Sense: *Able to understand or reason something out*

Sparse: *Limited*

Termite: *A social insect that eats wood*

Wander: *To move from place to place without purpose or a known destination*

Warned: *To tell someone about something that might cause harm or injury*

CHAPTER 8

The Village of No Roofs

Buddy Bear and his companion, Sly Fox, had just spent the night on the west side of some large buttes located in the middle of the Dangerous Desert. They didn't know yet that they had crossed half the distance of the desert, but they were about to find out.

Buddy was sound asleep, enjoying his peaceful rest in the shade of the rock formations, when Sly the Fox nudged him awake. "Time to be on our way," she announced. "We are not free of this cursed land; not yet. We must press on if we are ever to escape this infernal heat." What she was saying, in her own British style, was that it was time to get up and get going.

"Darn!" mumbled Buddy. "And I was finally getting some good rest." But he got up anyway.

Putting the buttes to their left, they began working their way around the south side of the massive obstacles. As they walked, they speculated as to what they would find. Who made the fire that made the smoke they saw from so far away? It had to be a big fire to make that much smoke. Why would anyone need such a big fire? What were their chances of getting some food? Would the people welcome them? All good questions. All without answers.

They talked about the people they had already met, and since everything in Mangonel seemed so strange, they had no idea what to expect on the east side of the massive rocks.

Just as Sly predicted, it took all day to go around the buttes. In the evening light they saw some buildings in the distance to the north. Buddy wanted to continue on so they could get to the town as soon as possible. Sly thought it wiser to wait until morning. Again, they were just too tired to be prepared for any new situation. In the end, they chose to wait until dawn the next day.

As the evening got darker, they watched as the windows in all the houses began to light up. It looked like every house had a fireplace, and all of them were being lit. Strange as it may seem, there was also a light shining up through the top of each building. Smoke was rising in swirling soft plumes from every house. The dwellings were close together, and the smoke from each of them joined together in the sky as it went up and up. This was definitely the source of the smoke Buddy and Sly had spotted from many miles away.

The next morning, the sun rose in the east. It made the day as hot as ever. The buttes blocked any wind that may have come from the west. No breeze caused it to seem even hotter. As they traveled closer to the buildings, they realized this was a small place, not big enough to be a town but large enough to be called a village.

Buddy and Sly went into the village while the residents sleepily stirred from their beds. One man came out of his front door. He immediately spotted the two newcomers strolling down the street. He quickly turned back into his house. In seconds he returned; only now, he was carrying a big gun. "Halt," he shouted. He turned his head back toward the door and yelled to his wife, "Mable, please go get the others." Soon Buddy and Sly were surrounded by men with guns.

Sly was first to say something, "Now gentlemen, you just contain some of your anxiety. We are friendly and mean you no harm. All we seek is information, and perchance, a cool drink."

The man who first saw them must have been the leader because he spoke again while the others stood still with their guns pointed. "Here is the information we will give you. Get out while the getting is good!"

Sly, for such a small creature, had a great deal of courage. She was also very confident in her ability to think through most problems. With a big smile, and her paws spread wide to show she was welcoming their friendship, she began again. "Why are you so opposed to letting us stay for a short time? We will be moving on as soon as we are rested. In fact, we will want to leave as soon as possible. We have goals of our own to meet. Furthermore, we wish not to be detained in this desert any longer than necessary. So, you see, we will be of little burden to you."

"Right," spat the man, "That is what they all say. Then they stay and stay and stay. While they're here, they eat all our food and drink our water, neither of which we have to spare. Very few come to our village. We like it that way. Nobody else likes it way out here in this desert, but when they get lost and find us, they want to take everything we have. We don't want any strangers to upset the balance of our lives anymore, so please, just go. As the appointed mayor of this village, I am sorry to say, you must leave."

Sly was thinking the entire time the man was talking. She was coming up with her own arguments. "Sir, if we promised to leave before noon, wouldn't that be acceptable?"

"Sure," said the mayor. "But what happens when you don't?"

Sly adopted a slightly harsher tone. "Are you saying I am a liar? Are you assuming I will not keep my word? Do you think we want to stay here with such unfriendly people, especially those who threaten us with guns?" Sly turned to Buddy, and with a wink, she said in a voice loud enough for the people to hear, "Come, Buddy, we will leave this place. We will tell everyone we meet on our journey that the people in this desert village are cruel to strangers in need of help."

"Wait," pleaded the leader. "We aren't mean; we are just trying to protect what little we have. We are kind to those who don't abuse our generosity and are very open to those who need help. Put down your guns, men." He leaned forward and whispered in Sly's ear, "I am sorry about the guns. We use them to hunt for food. Sometimes we use them to scare people away when we feel there will be trouble." Looking at Buddy, he said, "You are a very big bear, and there are no bears in the desert. You looked rather frightening, not to mention suspicious." He then put out his hand in friendship as he introduced himself. "I am called Luke the Duke. I am the appointed mayor of this village. Won't you please come into the house, have a drink of cool water, and rest a bit?"

They all went into the mayor's house, where the travelers were shocked to see there was no roof. Buddy Bear's look must have revealed his thoughts because Luke the Dude began to explain before either Buddy or Sly could ask their question. "This village is exactly in the middle of the desert. It's the driest place in the kingdom of Mangonel. What little rain that comes from the west is blocked by the buttes, so we get no rain, ever. Without rain, there is no need for roofs. We get to sleep under the stars every night, and we get the full benefit of any breeze that comes along. We also save on building materials, which are scarce, and the smoke from our fireplaces goes up and out of the house with ease. So you see, we have no need for roofs here."

"How clever," Sly remarked. "But if it never rains, where do you get your water?"

"The rain clouds come from the west. They are blocked by the buttes long before they reach us. When we see the dark sky, we rush to the west side and gather as much water as we can."

Buddy continued the questioning. "Then why not relocate your houses to the west side of the buttes where there is water?" he asked.

The mayor looked at Buddy as if he had no brains at all. "If we move to the west, we will need to build roofs. Besides, the evening sun is much hotter than the morning sun. Here, on the east side of the buttes, the sun is blocked from around noon all the way until it sets. We can live here, but on the west side we would all die from the heat."

All this time, the mayor and his wife were offering water to drink and some food to eat. Buddy and Sly were careful not to take too much. Then Sly said she thought she could help the village people. She told the mayor she had a plan. This is what she offered: "Here is an idea for you. Why not take your people to the topmost spot on the buttes where rain falls and dig a deep pit? Toward the top of the pit, dig a tunnel out to the east side of the buttes. This will channel any excess gathered water down toward the village. At the base of the channel, dig another large pit where the rain water can collect and be stored for when you need it. In this way you will have a reservoir at the top of the butte and one right near the village."

Luke the Duke thought this was such a great idea he suggested it to the people. The entire village felt Buddy and Sly had helped them so much, and they asked if they would like to be permanent residents. The visitors knew this was not going to happen. They had planned and promised to leave at noon that very day, and they intended to keep their promise.

At noon on the dot, Buddy and Sly announced their departure to the mayor and his wife, Mable. Mable asked where their provisions bag was so she could fill it for them. Buddy admitted they didn't have one, and neither did he know what it was. Mable disappeared into a back room. They could hear her rummaging around as she tried to find something. Minutes later she came out with a carpetbagger looking sack. It was large, with soft sides, and it opened at the top between two arched handles. On the outside were some markings, a lightning bolt on one side, and a crescent moon on the other. It was bulging at the sides. From its appearance, it looked to be filled to the brim.

"Here," she said. "It is the least we can do to repay you for the wonderful idea on how to get a constant water supply to our village. The bag is full of everything you will need while on your journey. Open it when you find yourself wanting something you cannot find by yourselves. Never take anything from the bag just to make things easy. Taking what you really do not need removes that item from your bag forever. We have stored enough firewood for the entire town to last us many, many years, and you have solved our water problem, so we no longer have any real need for the bag."

Buddy couldn't piece together what the bag had to do with firewood, but he accepted the bag without question. He hefted the sack up, surprised at how light it was. He hooked the handles over his shoulders, like a backpack, and it immediately settled into a comfortable position. The big bag had hardly any weight at all. What could possibly be in this sack when it weighed so little? Not wanting to go back on their promise, and after finding out they were at the halfway point, they were anxious to be on their way. They said their good-byes, offered a sincere thank you, and were soon trudging toward the east again.

That night, while they were gazing up at the stars, Buddy said to Sly, "What an interesting place Mangonel is. Back on earth none of the animals or trees can talk. Here everyone understands everything I say, and I understand them. Here I have all these great adventures. Back in Colorado I had lots of chores and only pretend adventures in the park." He paused for a spell, and then he asked a question he knew no one could answer. "I wonder how my mother is doing with me not there to help." He shook the idea from his head before it made him sad and asked Sly, "I wonder what adventures we'll find tomorrow. What will we encounter on the other side of this desert?"

"Be quiet. It's time to get some rest. I believe we have many more cruel days ahead of us in this infernal desert before we can dream of more pleasant ones," was Sly's reply. Then, after a moment, she added, "Good night, my dear friend. Sleep well."

Dictionary—Chapter 8

Abuse: *Mistreat*

Acceptable: *Considered to be satisfactory*

Anxiety: *Nervous concern*

Appointed: *Selected or chosen*

Assuming: *Expecting, believing something before it happens*

Balance: *Harmony, a reasonable state of steadiness*

Burden: *A difficult or worrisome responsibility*

Channel: *A long, narrow passage along which a liquid can flow*

Confident: *Certain, self-assured*

Contain: *To have or hold something inside*

Courage: *The ability to face a difficulty or danger and overcome the fear*

Cursed: *Afflicted with harm thought to be a result from a curse*

Departure: *The action of setting off on a journey*

Detained: *To hold back or to delay*

Dwellings: *Houses or buildings where people live*

Gazing: *To look at something for a long time*

Generosity: *Willingness to give money, help, or time freely*

Heft: *To lift something up*

Infernal: *Extremely annoying or unpleasant*

Intended: *A plan for the future*

Massive: *Very large, solid, and heavy*

Nudge: *To push or poke somebody gently*

Obstacles: *Things that are in the way*

Opposed: *To disagree*

Provisions: *Supply of something*

Relocate: *To move to a new place*

Reservoir: *A large supply of something, like water*

Residents: *Persons who live in a place for a long time*

Reveal: *To make something known or visible that was previously hidden*

Scarce: *An insufficient supply of an item, not enough*

Sincere: *Honest and based on a deeply felt truth*

Source: *The place or person from where something began*

Speculate: *To think of possibilities and other outcomes*

Surround: *To occupy the space around something*

Suspicious: *Inclined or tending to believe something is wrong*

CHAPTER 9

Out of the Desert

There were few things Buddy Bear and Sly Fox could not cope with, but the heat of the Dangerous Desert surely pressed them to their limit. Having crossed halfway and circled some large buttes, they visited with the people in the Village of No Roofs. It was a little shaky at first, but it all turned out well in the end. Buddy was given what Mable, the mayor's wife, called a provisions bag. It was full to the point of bursting, but she gave strict instructions to open it only when Buddy and Sly were incapable of finding what they needed on their own and could not obtain it by any other means.

On the third day after leaving the Village of No Roofs, Buddy and Sly were famished. Their hunger was evident by the constant growling in their stomachs. They looked for more termite hills, ants, beetles, lizards—anything to give them nourishment. Water was a problem too. Buddy had discovered if he dug a deep enough hole he could find water. The problem was, in this part of the desert, the water was just too deep to find.

They were settling down for the night when Sly commented on their predicament. "Another day with no water and no food to nourish us. I am getting dizzy from the lack of sustenance. My friend, we can last but a few more unpleasant days without nourishment, but without water, we may not survive through tomorrow."

Buddy slowly pulled the provisions bag from his shoulders and placed it on the ground. It had already become routine for him. He thought little of it. It was just a bag he had to carry and was forbidden to look inside. That is when Sly walked over to Buddy and snatched the satchel from him.

"We were instructed not to open this bag until we needed something we could not locate through our own efforts. I would submit this is just such an occasion. Let's see what secrets are contained in this bag." With that, she unfastened the flap and slowly peeked in. Then she threw it all the way open. Both Buddy and Sly were shocked at what they saw, or to be more accurate, what they didn't see. The pack was empty. Buddy closed the flap. He lifted the provisions bag high over his head, ready to heave it out into the dusty desert, never to carry it again. Then he set it back down. He couldn't believe Mable would have played such a dirty trick on them. He decided it was worth one last look. This time, when he opened the bag, he noticed a note attached to the top flap. He tore off the note, sat down, and read it aloud to Sly.

"This provision bag is known to some as a 'super sack'; others call it a 'Merlin's bag,' and some call it an 'impossible pack.'

The bag is full of everything imaginable, and anything you desire can be drawn from the sack by calling into the bag while reaching in to get it. Guard this with care. Only three of these were ever created. Even so, everyone in Mangonel knows of them, and this may be the last surviving bag."

Sly looked at Buddy, and Buddy looked at Sly. "Let's give it a go, shall we?" inquired the fox.

"What should we ask for?"

Sly answered almost before Buddy finished, "Request water and food for the two of us. Now, by Jove, get on with it. Why are you hesitating?"

"Maybe we should look around some more. I don't want to have all the water and food taken from the sack. What if we need more later on?"

"We have searched these past three days. Isn't that sufficient?"

"Yes, I suppose so," replied Buddy as he reluctantly gave in to her request. He put his hand in the bag and felt nothing. He was skeptical, but he also knew there were many oddities in the kingdom of Mangonel. He poked his face into the bag and called, "We would like some food and water because we are hungry and thirsty. If you ha …" Before he could finish, something slammed into his paw. He snatched it before it could fall back in. When he pulled his paw out, he was holding a large picnic basket. Inside, there were cooked chicken salad and tuna salad sandwiches, fresh carrots and celery, fresh fruits and berries, and there was a large jug of water for them to drink. There was even a cloth for them to spread out on the ground so they could eat without all the desert sand getting into the food. Each time they reached into the basket for another sandwich, another one was there for the taking. When they wanted more water, another jug was waiting for them.

After stuffing themselves, they lay back on the cloth and enjoyed the comfortable feeling of having full bellies again. "It would be wonderful to savor an ice cream cone at this time," dreamed Sly. Buddy reached in the basket and called for two ice cream cones. He had to grab quickly or he would have missed them, but sure enough, there, in the middle of the desert, were two ice cold ice cream cones for them to enjoy.

They finished their dessert and packed all the wrappings and jugs into the basket. Then they folded the cloth and placed it neatly on top. Buddy opened the provisions bag and started pushing the basket back in. It was a tight fit, but it was going back in, little by little. On the last push, the entire basket dropped into the bag with a *whoosh*. Buddy gazed in to see how it could even fit in there, but the provisions bag was once again empty. This certainly was a valuable bag. Buddy vowed he would never let anyone else touch it or reach inside.

Full of delicious food, and no longer thirsty, the partners turned to the east and began walking once more. It was a wonderful feeling knowing that if they truly needed something they could not get for themselves, the provisions bag was there to help them along. Virtually everything was at their disposal. It was like the comforting feeling you get from a favorite blanket or knowing your parents are always there when you need them. Even in this hot, dry desert, Buddy and Sly were very content.

Several more days passed in the terrible heat, but at no time did the two friends use the provisions bag again. Acting responsibly, they tried to make do with what they had so the bag would not discard the items because of their abuse of the privilege.

During their trek from the Land of No Roofs, and on their way out of the Dangerous Desert, they discovered the days to be exceedingly hot and the nights very cold. The great change in temperature made the difference seem even more extreme. At some point, they found themselves reversing their order of travel. That was a big help. They were now traveling at night when the air was cooler and sleeping during the day when it was too hot to travel. There were, however, a couple of drawbacks to this reversal. One problem was that when there was no moon, they couldn't see very well. Another problem was they couldn't sleep well in the heat of the day.

One morning, just before making camp, Buddy put Sly on his shoulders to have a look around. Sly had to strain her eyes to see, but she was sure she could see trees in the distance. Sly told Buddy about the trees, but she warned they might be a mirage, like all the little shiny lakes they had seen disappear as they got closer. Without saying another word, the two prepared their camp. They tried very hard to fall asleep so they would be ready to carry on when the stars came out. (Forced sleep never works because the more you try to sleep, the more you stay awake.) They were so excited about getting out of the desert that they tossed and turned the entire day.

At that wonderful time, just before sunset, the two got up and began what they hoped would be their final night in that wasteland. They watched the sun go down in a blaze of magnificent colors as it hid behind the horizon. To the east, the sky was a beautiful robin's egg blue. All of the clouds were fluffy puffs of white. The edges of the clouds were trimmed in silver and red. To the west, the sun dropped slowly. The closer it got to the horizon, the more dramatic the colors of the sky became. The horizon was glowing with reds, oranges, and yellows. All the clouds were rimmed with bright edges, lit up from the sun's rays as they changed shape. The little puffs had been blown into long streaks, which were now spread out across the sky like ribs in a giant fan. What a glorious night this was.

Even after the sun had set, they could see pretty well. The moon and stars lit the terrain enough for them to notice the trees becoming more defined. They now knew it was no mirage. They also knew they were finally headed out of this dangerous place. That thought made them abundantly happy. By midnight, they stepped out of the moonlight and into the dark space under the smaller trees that belted the forest. It was best to stop here and wait for the sun to come up. It would be far too dark in the forest to travel at night. If they continued, someone was bound to get hurt.

When the morning sun rose in the sky, the forest remained dark. There were thick clouds overhead. Adding to the darkness were the trees of the inner forest. They were so high and thick, they nearly blocked out all the sun. Neither Buddy nor Sly had ever seen such tall trees. Every so often there would be a break in the dark clouds that formed over the huge trees. They could see the forest was denser than any forest they had ever seen. Even when the sun shone brightly, it was still dark under the thick leaves that were crowded together on every branch. Every time the clouds returned, it would rain for a few minutes. Then the clouds would break up and move on. There was no end to this cycle. This was going to be another weird experience in the land of Mangonel. Buddy and Sly were both leery of going much farther into the dark unknown that lie before them.

Buddy swallowed hard and turned to Sly, "What do you think about spending another night here, closer to the edge? Maybe the weather will be more cooperative tomorrow. Besides, it will give us a chance to form a plan on how to tackle this new adventure."

"Splendid idea," Sly agreed. She was thinking the same thing but didn't want Buddy to know how frightened she was.

Buddy had grown a lot larger during his time in Mangonel, but he still had no idea how big he was. To him, he was just the same Buddy Bailey, now a bear cub, and he was still afraid of silly things, like what might be waiting for them in the darkness of the forest.

They settled in for the day and another night. Buddy scrunched up the provisions bag. To keep it safe, he put it under his head like a pillow. It was uncomfortable, but he wasn't going to take any chances of losing it or having someone run off with it while he rested. There were things out there in the forest, he just knew it. His bear senses told him so. As the night got progressively darker, he could almost feel eyes looking at them, staring at them.

Buddy tried to think of how nice and cool and comfortable this night was compared to the desert. He thought of all the adventures he had already experienced in Mangonel. He also thought of all the new adventures that were waiting in the days ahead. In time, he fell fast asleep, dreaming of wonderful things that were to come.

Dictionary—Chapter 9

Abundant: *Having more than enough, present in great quantities*

Abuse: *Mistreatment*

Cooperative: *Helpful and supportive of someone else*

Cope: *To deal with something that is difficult*

Defined: *The clear edge of something*

Denser: *Thicker than something else*

Desire: *To want something very strongly*

Disposal: *Close to hand and ready for use*

Drawbacks: *Hindrances, things that get in the way of doing something*

Drawn: *Pulled toward, to be taken from or out of something*

Evident: *Easy and clear to see and understand*

Famished: *Very hungry*

Glorious: *Very lovely, beautiful*

Heave: *Throw something, also to drag, pull, yank, or tug on something*

Hesitating: *To pause or be slow in doing something*

Horizon: *The line in the farthest distance where the land meets the sky*

Incapable: *Lacking the ability or strength needed to do something*

Imaginable: *Possible, able to be thought of; as in using one's imagination*

Immense: *Great in size, huge*

Instructions: *To tell someone to do something or how to do it*

Leery: *To be suspicious, untrusting of someone or something*

Locate: *To find something*

Magnificent: *Something that is wonderful*

Means: *Something that is available and makes it possible to do something*

Mirage: *An illusion*

Nourishment: *Food*

Oddities: *Somebody or something unusual or unique*

Occasion: *A point in time; time and circumstance create occasions*

Predicament: *A difficult or embarrassing situation with no clear way out*

Privilege: *An advantage or benefit*

Progressively: *Growing, developing over a period of time*

Reluctantly: *Feeling no willingness to do something*

Reversing: *Doing something in an opposite way*

Rimmed: *An outer edge that surrounds something*

Routine: *Usual practice*

Savor: *To enjoy something slowly and appreciatively*

Scrunch: *To pull and push something tightly together.*

Skeptical: *Not inclined to believe something*

Snatched: *Quickly grabbed something*

Splendid: *Excellent, perfect*

Submit: *To suggest an idea, to hand someone something*

Sufficient: *Enough, as much as is needed*

Sustenance: *Food, water; nourishment*

Terrain: *Ground or a piece of land*

Trek: *To make a long, difficult journey*

Valuable: *Something that has great worth or is precious*

Virtually: *Nearly; almost but not quite*

Vowed: *Pledged, promised with all intentions to fulfill the promise made*

CHAPTER 10

The Great Rain Forest of Mangonel

Finally, the Dangerous Desert was behind them. Buddy Bear and Sly Fox awoke in the pleasant shade of the trees rimming a huge forest. Buddy donned his provisions bag as he had done so many times, for so many days. He approached Sly to nudge her awake for yet a new experience in the Kingdom of Mangonel.

"Hey, the sun is up. You should be too," Buddy called to his friend. "It looks like we are in for a cool day for a change."

"I do believe you are correct, Mr. Bear," Sly mumbled with a yawn as she stretched to get the kinks out. "Are we to continue due east, or do you have another destination in mind at this juncture?"

"No, no," uttered Buddy. "I plan to keep going east until we can go no more. Then we will decide which direction we should explore next. I decided long ago the best plan would be to not just jump around. If we do that, we will never know if we have searched all the possibilities. There has to be a pattern."

"Quite so," observed Sly. "Then let's be off." With that said, she began stepping over the fallen twigs and branches as they entered the much darker part of the forest.

Once they were in the forest, they weren't sure of their exact heading (the direction they were traveling) because the massive trees nearly blocked out the sun completely. Buddy had climbed trees before to see which way to go. He thought he should try this method again. Up, up, up he climbed. Then he came across the strangest thing. There were roots entwined throughout the upper limbs of the tree tops. Snaking his way through the tangled mess, Buddy discovered another layer of trees growing on top of the trees that came up from the ground. With two layers of tree leaves, combined with the mess of jumbled roots in the upper branches, it was no wonder why it was so dark down on the ground.

By the time Buddy reached the elevated root system, he was already a hundred or more feet in the air. The second layer of trees was almost as tall as the one he had just climbed. Up this high, there was a stiff breeze that made the entire upper forest swing and sway. Buddy was afraid to go any higher, so he returned to the ground to tell Sly all about what he had found.

Buddy could hardly contain his excitement. "There are trees growing on top of trees. When I got to the highest limbs of this tree, I found myself in the roots of another. When I wiggled through the roots I found trees, just as big as these on the ground, growing on top, sort of piggyback style. Can you believe it?"

"That explains everything," remarked the fox. "We must have entered a rain forest. The small storms that keep forming above, the extra foliage in the canopy, and the darkness and dampness on the ground are all similar to that of a rain forest. The canopy here must be very thick to grow trees, but growing plants and such in the treetops is fairly common under these conditions. This puts my mind at ease. I feel so much better knowing what we are facing rather than trekking about into some unknown." Sly then added one last comment with a bit of a smile on her face. "Fear not, good fellow, I am familiar with these hostile conditions, and I know what is required for surviving in a rain forest."

"Hostile conditions," gasped Buddy. "What hostile conditions?"

"As long as you do not eat what I tell you not to eat and you do not touch what I tell you not to touch, we will be rather comfortable nestled in these trees," offered the fox. "There are plants that are poisonous, and there are frogs and snakes that are poisonous as well. On earth I can identify many of the plants that may cause problems. Here, I am not so sure. Generally, all insects and snakes that are brightly colored are poisonous in some form. Their bright colors are a sort of warning to leave them alone. If you are ever unsure, it is best just to stay clear of it. If you will follow me, we will be just fine."

"I am right behind you," Buddy stated, gulping. He would not take another step until the fox led the way.

The forest was an array of deep, dark greens. Every once in a while the sun would find an opening in the overhead branches, casting a beam of light down to the forest floor. Buddy would look up each time, because the green leaves would all become vibrant shades, ranging from bright yellow to deep turquoise. It was beautiful, and Buddy appreciated beautiful things. In his mind, there was always time to stop and take in the wonders of life and the beauty that surrounded him. If he didn't take the time to enjoy the experiences when they presented themselves, he might miss his chance forever.

The traveling pair spent many weeks in the rain forest. There was plenty to eat, little freshwater streams were everywhere, the forest floor was smooth and soft to walk on, and there was no reason to hurry on to some other unknown destination. Traveling here in the forest was far better than in the desert; however, there were some unpleasant features of the forest.

There was a definite lack of sunshine, and the constant rain was annoying. The rain was not so bad at first, but every day, three, four, five times a day it would rain. When the rain stopped, the air would become hot and humid. Merely breathing would make them perspire. Just about the time the forest became comfortable, it would rain again, but there was one more thing that bothered Buddy, and it bothered him more than anything else. He never could rid himself of the feeling of being watched.

After a few weeks, Buddy and Sly became accustomed to the rainy weather. When it looked like rain was coming, they would grab an enormous leaf from one of the plants and sit under it while they waited for the clouds to pass.

Every day the two friends would pick a direction and start exploring that area of the forest. There was so much to see. There were wild pigs that snorted in the dirt, trying to find roots to eat, but they were not very nice. They charged at Buddy and Sly when they got too close. There were many brightly colored insects, spiders, and snakes, and just as Sly had instructed, Buddy gave them all plenty of room. The trees were full of birds, singing and chirping, competing with one another to see which one had the nicest song. Fast-swinging monkeys and slow-moving sloths roamed the forest trees. It was a great deal noisier in this rain forest than Buddy thought it would be.

Buddy took to searching for as many different birds as he could find. People call this bird-watching; Buddy called it fun. He found finches and crows, robins and blue jays, mockingbirds and doves, cardinals and blackbirds, cockatoos and crows, but the ones he loved the most were the brightly colored parakeets and parrots.

One parrot Sly and Buddy stumbled upon could talk as well as whistle. He could say all sorts of things, like "Hello," and "My name is Jasper," and "How are you?" But he didn't have the ability to have a conversation. He needed to be trained, and there was nobody around to train him. They played with that parrot for hours. That certainly was an interesting day.

Every now and then, there was that gnawing feeling that they were being watched—a sensation that there was someone just out of sight, keeping an eye on what Sly and Buddy were doing. One afternoon Buddy caught a glimpse of something shiny in the bushes. His peripheral vision had picked up a glimmer that made him turn quickly to see what it was, but the thing was gone. It could have been just a glint of sunlight, but he was sure it was not. Whatever it was, it was very fast and very secretive. Buddy pledged to keep his eyes open so he could get a better look the next time it showed itself.

The longer they stayed in the rain forest, the more frequent the glimpses of shimmering light appeared, and the length of time it was visible grew ever so slightly longer. Whatever it was, it seemed to be getting more comfortable with a bear and a fox in the woods.

In the early morning of one particular day, Buddy caught a peek of the shiny thing again, and then there was a loud sound of something bursting. *Pop*! It sounded like bursting bubble gum. There was only one pop, followed by complete silence.

Ever so carefully Buddy made his way over to where the sound had come from. He peered around one tree, and then another, and another, but he never saw anyone or anything. Behind one tree, there was a puddle of shimmering goo on the ground that was quickly turning to liquid. Buddy touched it. It was slimy and slippery in his paw. It felt like soap that had been sitting in water too long. The substance, although strange, smelled very nice, like flowers.

"Please don't hurt me," came a tiny plea from a hidden being.

"I can't even see you," said Buddy. "And I wouldn't hurt you unless you intend to hurt me. Come out where I can see you. Then we can talk."

From behind a scraggly shrub, not at all where Buddy was looking, stepped a smallish, round-faced boy. He was a roly-poly little guy with plump cheeks, and skin as white as snow. It was obvious he wasn't very strong, and he appeared to be rather vulnerable out here in the forest all alone. Buddy tried to be calm and reassuring. "I am a bear, and my name is Buddy Bailey, I mean, Buddy Bear. The fox over there by that tree is Silvia, but you may call her Sly. We are not of the kingdom of Mangonel. We are only passing through until we find a way back to our home. Perhaps you can help us."

The boy slowly became more relaxed in the presence of the large bear. Soon he began to talk. He spoke in a high-pitched voice, "My name is Justin. I'm a Bubbler. I live in a town hidden deep in this rain forest. I burst my bubble. Now I have to go home and ask my mother to get me another. She is going to be upset with me because this is the third one I've burst this week." Then he brightened. "Hey!" he exclaimed. "Maybe you could go with me. When everyone sees you, they might forget about me and all the bubbles I broke."

Buddy asked, "Have you been spying on us?"

"Oh, yes," Justin confessed. "I have come to watch you nearly every day since you first arrived."

"Why didn't you come out and speak with us?" inquired Sly. "Why did you feel the need to spy on us at all?"

"What was all that goo you left on the ground?" Buddy added.

"We have lived in this forest for a long time. Our survival depends on us being very careful. To protect our people from all the rain, our scientists have been perfecting a way to keep us dry. Many, many years ago, my ancestors learned how to make large, strong bubbles that allow us to go where we like without getting wet. In order to help keep our bubble-protected village safe, I kept watch over you to make sure you were friendly. If I thought you were going to cause any trouble, I would have gone to warn the village. You see, you are the reason I have recently popped so many bubbles. This part of the forest has a lot of sharp objects, and they keep puncturing my personal bubbles." Justin took a deep breath before pressing on. "You guys are partly to blame for all my trouble, so will you please come to the village with me and help me explain what has happened?"

Buddy and Sly had many more questions to ask. With nowhere else to go, they agreed to follow the boy to his home. Each of them had their own thoughts as to what kind of adventure this was going to lead to.

Dictionary—Chapter 10

Accustomed: *Familiar, usual*

Ancestors: *Very old relatives*

Annoying: *Causing mild anger*

Appreciate: *To recognize or like somebody or something*

Array: *A wide range of something*

Canopy: *The uppermost layer of vegetation in a forest, forming a kind of ceiling*

Competing: *To try to win or do something better than others*

Donned: *To put something on*

Elevated: *Raised above the surrounding ground, a higher elevation*

Enormous: *Unusually large, great in size*

Features: *A part of something that makes it special*

Foliage: *The leaves of plants*

Glint: *A gleam or a flash*

Gnawing: *Persistent and troubling*

Identify: *To recognize, to know*

Juncture: *At this point in time*

Lack: *A complete absence of a particular thing*

Merely: *No more than is necessary*

Method: *A certain alternative way*

Nudge: *To push or shove someone gently*

Nestle: *To settle into a position that feels comfortable*

Observe: *To see or notice something*

Particular: *Relating to one person or thing out of several*

Peer: *To look at something very carefully*

Perspire: *Sweat*

Peripheral: *At the edge of something*

Pledge: *A solemn promise*

Presence: *A physical existence of something in a particular location and time*

Presented: *To be offered something*

Puncturing: *To have a small hole in something*

Rain Forest: *A large area covered in trees and plants growing close together*

Ranging: *Covering a number of similar things*

Reassuring: *Having the effect of making people feel more comfortable, less worried*

Rimming: *An outer edge, usually slightly raised*

Scraggly: *Messy and uneven in appearance*

Secretive: *Unwilling to reveal information*

Sloth: *A slow-moving mammal*

Trekking: *To make a long and difficult journey*

Turquoise: *A greenish blue color*

Vibrant: *Having a full, rich color or sound*

Vulnerable: *In a position where someone or something can be easily harmed*

CHAPTER 11

The Bubblers

Buddy's suspicions of being watched while he and Sly traveled were confirmed when he found a young boy. The curious fellow had been spying on the two travelers from the first day they had entered the Great Rain Forest of Mangonel. The boy said his name was Justin. He explained that he was a Bubbler from a village hidden deep in the rain forest, and now he was going to be in trouble because he needed a new bubble.

Buddy and Sly agreed to follow Justin home with the intention of helping him explain why he had popped yet another precious bubble. The journey through the rain forest was easy with Justin as their guide. He knew every path, every shortcut, and every direction he needed to take to get wherever he wanted in this forest. He was not as vulnerable as Buddy had first imagined.

It didn't take long before they were standing in front of a massive half bubble that covered an entire village. The enclosure was perfectly clear, like glass, allowing Buddy and

Sly to plainly see the village nestled inside. All of the villagers were scampering about cleaning the large bubble's surface and doing other odd jobs that normally have to be done to a home and within a village. They all, except the littlest children, were dressed in white and carried sacks over their shoulder. Buddy asked their new friend what the sacks contained.

Justin explained, "The sacks carry a personal bubble in case of an emergency, like the main bubble popping or when someone wants to leave the main enclosure, like I do. Whenever people go outside the big dome, they get into their own personal bubbles to protect themselves from the rain."

Buddy and Sly were shown the way into the main enclosure without causing it to burst. They trailed behind the boy as he walked along the village streets leading them to his house. The people acted like it was normal to see a bear walking down the road. Nobody spoke to them as they traveled through the carefully maintained streets. They merely waved a pleasant greeting and went about their business. Justin turned into a little property with a round house. In fact, all the houses were round; however, each one was different in some way. All of the homes were made from one or more dense bubbles, and they appeared to be made of the same mysterious material that formed the village covering. The only difference was you couldn't see through the house bubbles. Each dwelling was unique in some way. Some were a series of small bubbles set side by side on the ground. Some were placed one on top of another. Others were stacked to create odd and interesting forms. All of them were amazing.

Justin's house was two stories high. It had one large bubble resting on top of many smaller bubbles. Both the front door and all the windows were round. As the trio approached, Justin's mother was standing at the front door, and the way she was looking at him suggested she wasn't paying any attention to Buddy or Sly. Poor Justin was not going to get off easy for breaking another bubble. His mother stared at him and then asked him to show her his bubble. Obviously, he couldn't do that since it was nothing but a pile of goo in the forest.

"Mom," Justin began, "I have some new friends I would like you to meet. Buddy Bear and Sly Fox. They made sure I got home safely after my bubble burst outside. I thought it would be nice to have them stay with us tonight because they were so kind to me."

Buddy and Sly looked at each other with questioning glances. The kid had stretched the story a bit, but they were not going to have Justin punished for his curiosity. Besides, he was a nice kid, and the two companions liked him.

After Justin's mother gave him a stern look, she said that it would be fine for Buddy and Sly to stay as long as they didn't mind sleeping in the yard behind the house. It was then they noticed the temperature was just perfect inside the big enclosure, and there was exactly the right amount of humidity. Not one person looked to be uncomfortable, no matter what the weather was doing in the rainy forest. Buddy took a look toward the sky, and sure enough, it had begun raining again, but the big bubble was keeping everyone dry as toast. Buddy looked at Sly; she too was looking at the large protective dome.

Sly stood with her mouth open as she gazed upward. Buddy looked at Justin's mother, and while pointing up to the sky, he questioned, "How do you do that? How do you make these marvelous bubbles?" Speaking to the woman, he noticed his voice was changing to a much higher pitch. He was beginning to sound like Justin.

Justin's mother took her small personal bubble from her pouch and handed it to Buddy so he could examine it. "The bubbles," she said, "are made from the moisture in the air. Water is very dense; even though you cannot walk on it in its natural state, if you condense it, or freeze it, it gets very hard indeed. What we do is force the surrounding moisture into an area of our choosing. We can make any shape or size we like as long as there is enough water in the air. Round is the easiest and most useful shape of all, so we make bubbles. Since we need water to make the bubbles, the rain forest is the perfect place for us to live. Although we do not like the rain, we need it for our enclosures. The bubbles, even the large village dome, are nothing more than moisture condensed into a specific area, creating a shield. The area inside is filled with a special kind of air our scientists have discovered. The gas is combined with oxygen and is very light. The light gas floats to the edges of our enclosures and helps to hold the condensed moisture in place. The new gas is called hemilin. No, that isn't correct. Healym. No, helium. Yes, that's it, helium. The gas makes us all speak with squeaky voices, but that is a small price to pay. You too will have a high-pitched voice while you are here. Once you leave, your voices will return to normal."

"How clever!" exclaimed Sly. "But you still didn't answer how you make the bubbles."

"That, my friends, is a very guarded secret. I cannot tell you, as I am not sure myself. We get our personal protection bubbles from the leader's camp, and they get them from the bubble maker's encampment. The bubble makers are sworn to secrecy, and they all work and live inside a specially protected area that is surrounded yet again by the leader's camp bubble. You see, not even the citizens know how it is done."

Buddy was still curious, "Okay, so why do you carry a small bubble in your pouch? It looks like it would be too small to fit anything." Then he remembered his provisions bag and felt silly for asking.

Still, the woman answered. "These small bubbles have enough material to produce an enclosure just the right size to fit one person. Each one can be inflated up to seven feet in diameter, so they can fit anyone who is carrying it. One size fits all, so to speak; except for you, Mr. Bear. You would not fit into a bubble—not even close. All one needs to do is stretch the bubble with a canister of gas, find the opening, which is marked in white glitter, and step in."

"Amazing," Sly exclaimed.

That night, the two travelers were invited to stay under the village dome, and they slept out in the little backyard behind Justin's home. It was one of the most comfortable nights they had had in the rain forest. It was warm and dry, and the grass had no dew on it at all. The splatter of rain on the bubble high over their heads made a soft sound that lulled them off to sleep as they lay quietly thinking their own private thoughts.

Buddy woke first. He yawned, stretched, and looked for his provisions bag. It was gone. "Oh, no!" Buddy growled.

That got Sly up and going in a hurry. "What's the matter?"

"The provisions bag, the Merlin's sack, or whatever you want to call it, is gone." Now Sly too was fully awake and worried they had lost their most prized possession. What were they to do?

Sly sprang into action in an instant. She was at the back door to Justin's house before Buddy could move a muscle. She banged on the door, and when the mother opened it, Sly said in the most polite voice she could manage, "My good and kind hostess, as we slept upon your lovely lawn last evening, someone absconded with our bag. It is very valuable to us, and we simply will not depart from this village until we retrieve it. Would you, or your family, have any idea where we might search for our missing property?"

The woman was in shock and apparently in as much surprise as she could be. "What! Something was taken from you?" she asked.

"Well, yes. I do believe that is what I just told you."

Justin's mother continued, "This is horrible. No one steals anything in this village. We're too small of a community to get away with stealing something. It would be known in an instant. How would you ever get away with it? Everyone would be looking for the object. If someone did steal something, it could never be used, so what would be the point?"

Interesting concept, thought Buddy. "If that's how everyone here thinks, what happened to our bag?"

Nobody could answer that question. Sly suggested they all begin to search for the bag, starting with the yard, and then branching out across the village. By this time, one of the neighbors was awake. He asked what all the commotion was about. After hearing the story of what had happened, he passed the word around the town. Soon, more people were searching, and before you knew it, the whole community was out trying to locate the missing bag.

Suddenly, while Buddy was looking off to his left, he was rammed in his belly by something. "Ooooooph!" was all he could utter. If he were not so large, he would have had the wind knocked out of him completely. Looking down, Buddy saw a smallish animal lying dazed at his feet. Alongside of it was their bag. Buddy picked up the provisions bag and yelled for everyone to pass the word that he found the bag, and they could stop searching. Next, he picked up the animal. It was a raccoon. It sort of stood to reason the thief would be someone who wore a mask.

Buddy waited while the raccoon revived himself from the collision. As the little creature started to show signs of consciousness, Buddy set him back on the ground. Buddy insisted the masked bandit tell everyone who he was and why he had stolen the bag. The raccoon shook his head to clear it, and said, "Hiya! Sorry, I don't really have a name. Most people tell me I am a bit pesky, whatever that is, so I guess that's my name, Pesky Raccoon. That is as good a name as any."

Sly chimed in. "Pesky surely fits your personality, Mr. Raccoon. Now as to why you took the bag?"

"Oh, I guess it's just in my nature. I saw the thing just lying about, and I couldn't resist picking it up. I didn't mean any harm, just curious. I had planned on returning it, but before I got around to giving it back, everyone started running about searching for the darn thing. I knew I was in trouble, so I just sort of hid until I thought I could put it back from where I got it, and nobody would be the wiser. The problem was, while I was running, *boom*, I ran into you."

"I know that part," said Buddy. "It seems everybody keeps running into my belly."

By now a crowd had gathered. They all wanted to know where the masked fellow had come from. There were no raccoons in the Land of the Bubblers. The bear and the fox had been accompanied by Justin. They appeared to have been invited, but this fellow …

Pesky was confused. He said he had been searching for some food in a garbage pile when he found a particularly large can that held a great deal of promise for an evening meal. When he went into the can, it got really dark. There seemed to be no bottom to it, catching everyone up to date. He then explained, "Next thing I knew I was in this forest climbing out from under a rock. When I saw you walking through the forest, I followed you. After you entered this shiny thing, I waited a minute or two, and then I walked in right behind you."

Another porthole into Mangonel, Buddy reflected.

All the townspeople didn't want a potential thief in their midst. They refused to let him stay inside the bubble. Someone picked him up and escorted him outside of the protection of the main dome. Meanwhile, Buddy and Sly were invited to stay as long as they wished.

Sly thought they had stayed long enough. After all, they had disturbed the entire village in just one morning. They gazed around at the faces of the people and offered their good-byes, as well as their sincere thanks. Then, with Justin in tow, they made their way to the bubble's exit port. As it turned out, they needed Justin as a guide because it was not easy to find the opening. Standing at the entrance, Justin expressed his desire to go with them. He loved an adventure. After all, that is why he kept going outside and bursting so many bubbles in the first place. Buddy and Sly both had to tell him he couldn't go this time; maybe he would be big enough the next time they came by this way. The boy was very sad. He told them they would be missed. There had not been so much excitement since the day the mayor broke the main cover with a firecracker.

Standing at the exit portal, Buddy and Sly each took a deep breath; then the partners looked at each other. In unison, they asked, "Where to now?"

Dictionary—Chapter 11

Absconded: *To run away from or with something*

Awe: *A feeling of amazement and respect mixed with fear*

Bearer: *Somebody who brings or carries something*

Canister: *A metal container with a lid for storing things*

Collision: *When two or more objects come in contact with one another*

Commotion: *Lots of noise and confusion*

Concept: *An idea somebody has thought up*

Condense: *To squeeze together something into a tighter, denser space*

Configuration: *The way the parts of something are put together*

Confirmed: *Having been found to be true*

Consciousness: *To be awake and aware of what is going on around you*

Contain: *To hold something inside*

Curiosity: *Eagerness to know something or to get information*

Dazed: *A state of confusion*

Dense: *So close together that there is little empty space*

Depart: *To leave, to go away from someplace*

Diameter: *A straight line that goes from one side of a circle to the other and through the center*

Distinctly: *Definite or undeniable*

Disturbed: *Worried or concerned*

Emergency: *An unexpected or sudden event*

Encampment: *The place where someone makes camp*

Enclosure: *A boundary, like a fence*

Escorted: *To be guided by one or more persons*

Glance: *To look at something quickly*

Helium: *A gas that is lighter than air, used to blow up balloons so they float*

Huge: *Very large*

Humidity: *Amount of moisture (water) in the air*

Horrible: *Very bad and unpleasant or unsightly*

Hostess: *A woman who invites or welcomes and entertains guests with food and drinks*

Inflate: *To expand with air, like a balloon*

Inhabitants: *Persons or animals that live in a particular area*

Interesting: *Attracting and holding attention*

Invitation: *An offer to come or to go someplace*

Lull: *To soothe or calm a person*

Marvelous: *Extraordinarily wonderful*

Midst: *To be in the middle of something*

Mysterious: *Difficult to understand*

Obviously: *Clearly, suggests there is no doubt*

Personality: *The total of someone's attitude, interests, behavior, and more*

Pesky: *Troublesome, irritating*

Pitch: *A specific or particular key, especially in music*

Polite: *Showing good manners*

Port: *An opening*

Porthole: *A round opening*

Potential: *A possibility for something to happen*

Produce: *To make or create something, to cause something to happen*

Rammed: *To strike something with great force*

Refused: *Decline, to say no*

Resist: *To hold back*

Retrieve: *To save something from being lost*

Revived: *To come back to life or regain strength or consciousness*

Scampering: *To run about playfully*

Scientist: *Someone who has studied the particulars of gas, matter, or other mysteries of nature*

Sincere: *Honest*

Structures: *Buildings, bridges, or other objects put together from many different parts*

Suspicion: *An idea that something is wrong but having no proof*

Sympathy: *To share someone else's feelings*

Trailed: *Followed behind*

Unison: *Doing the same thing at the same time*

Utter: *To say something*

Vulnerable: *Open to harm*

CHAPTER 12

A Run-In with Ralph

With the wave of one last good-bye to Justin, Sly and Buddy turned to exit the bubble, when …

"Oooooph!" Pesky, the raccoon who had taken their provisions bag, ran right into Buddy again.

The raccoon would not stop jabbering. "Boy oh boy! Am I glad to see you! I was afraid you were going to leave without me. I don't have any friends in this strange place, I have no place to go, and I am all alone. Could I come with you? Could I? Pretty please? I won't give you any more trouble. I'll just follow along behind you. Honest, I will. Please let me come along. I just need—"

Buddy held up his paw and cut the raccoon off midsentence. "Okay, okay! Just be quiet for a second, and stop running into me."

Then he looked at Sly, who stated, "We can offer the little guy a go, if it is all right with you."

Buddy pondered on it for a second or two. Finally they agreed to let the raccoon join them. However, there was one condition. Pesky had to promise not to steal anything from anyone. If he did, they would cast him out, just as the Bubblers had done. Pesky promised. He was so happy he ran around in a big circle trying to burn off all the excitement that had built up inside him.

"Where are we headed?" asked Pesky. "When are we going to arrive? How far away is it? Do you know—" Again, Buddy put his paw up to quiet the raccoon.

"His name sure fits him," Buddy whispered to Sly. She nodded in agreement. Buddy looked at their new companion and tried to be stern. "This is a quiet journey. You must try to be silent, or you will not fit in," he scolded as he winked at Sly.

Along the way they came across another traveler. He was very, very old. His beard was so long he had it wrapped around his neck like a scarf, and still it reached to his knees. Even though he was very old, he moved rather quickly. He spoke just as fast as he moved. Buddy asked the man if he knew the best way to go to get out of the rain forest. The odd fellow turned to look and point away from Buddy. He pointed his shaking finger to the south and rapidly replied. "Continue south to the river. That is the Rain Forest River. You can follow it out. It leads to the Giant Falls and connects with the River River on the left that leads due east. The river on the right is the South

River River. It leads south, just like its name implies. Now, if you don't mind, I, like you, am on a journey. I have little time to stand around and chat. If anyone asks, you can tell them you saw Rip—Rip Van Winkle. I am sure someone must be looking for me. I've been asleep for a long, long time." The fellow stopped talking, turned back to the direction he had been traveling, and marched off down the path.

Pesky remarked in a whisper, "What in Mangonel was that all about? The guy sure seemed in a hurry. Makes you wonder what's up ahead, doesn't it?" Buddy wasn't too worried. The old man they met was only a copy of the story of Rip Van Winkle. He was no more than just another oddity in the kingdom of Mangonel, nothing to fear.

They wandered around in the rain forest trying to find the Rain Forest River. Eventually they came across a small stream. This could be what Mr. Winkle was describing, so they decided to follow it downstream to see where it led them. It did run south, so they felt it couldn't hurt. As they traveled beside the stream, it grew larger. Soon it became a creek, and the creek grew to become a river. Sly suggested they should all get a log so they could float down the river. If this was the river the old man spoke of, they could float right out of the forest on the river's current. Riding on a log, they would save a great deal of energy. Not only would it be easier, but the trip would also be much faster than walking. Sly improved on her idea. She recommended they build a raft. A raft would offer more room, and they would stay dry.

They began gathering logs from the forest floor. Pesky was in charge of getting the strong, flexible vines to tie the logs together. With these materials they were going to fashion a raft to ride on. Buddy, as would be expected, gathered much larger logs than Sly. Pesky, who was supposed to gather up vines to be used as rope, did nothing but run up and down telling Buddy his logs were too big and Sly that hers were too small. "Pick this one. Now get that one. This one over here is just right," Pesky would say. Eventually Buddy and Sly both realized Pesky was picking all the logs of the same size. The raft would be much more comfortable with all matching logs and a whole lot easier to build. Pesky's idea seemed to be a good one, so Buddy and Sly gave in. They started picking up only the logs Pesky pointed out to them.

Gathering enough wood that matched in size took a lot longer, but it was necessary if they were to build a proper raft. The vines were easier to find, but building the raft was hard work. In the end, it all worked out perfectly. When finished, Sly got onto the raft first. As Buddy started to climb on, Pesky ran right through his legs and scampered onto the craft. Buddy wasn't ready for Pesky to zoom past him. Startled, Buddy jumped to the side. The big bear lost his balance, and *splash*, into the river he went. He huffed and puffed like the Big Bad Wolf as he climbed out of the water. He shook himself dry, and then he started to laugh and laugh and laugh. As he gasped for air, he said, "We built this raft to stay dry, and here I am, all wet." They all laughed until their sides hurt. When they had recovered from their giggling fits, Buddy shoved the raft off the bank as he climbed aboard. They were on their way for their first ride on a raft—a ride that would carry them on their way down the Rain Forest River.

Their cruise was very pleasant. They floated along on the flat water while the river's current carried them on their way. The water flowed south, wound left, then right, and then left again, making its way through the trees that crowded the banks. It didn't feel like they were going very fast, but when Pesky put his paw into the water, the pressure almost pulled him overboard.

Sly noticed how quickly the shoreline was passing. She cautioned her companions, "Hold on tight; I wager there is trouble ahead." Sure enough, just around the next bend they all heard the roar of the rapids. The river, crashing against the rocks and sunken logs, was causing an enormous racket. Everyone grabbed a loose vine and held on for dear life as the raft bounced up and down and back and forth, nearly tearing it to pieces as it was tossed to and fro over the many obstructions hidden under the water.

Suddenly, there was a pause in the churning water. It became perfectly calm again. They could still hear the roar of the rapids behind them, but they could also hear a roar coming from up ahead. "Oh boy, more rapids!" cheered Pesky, who apparently was enjoying himself through all the danger.

A minute or two later, they knew what was causing the roar. It was a waterfall. Buddy was not happy to know they were in the middle of the river with no paddles and heading toward a waterfall. Buddy, now a bear, wasn't sure he could swim. The river grew wider. It wasn't long before the current became too strong for them to swim to safety. There was nothing to do but to ride the raft down the waterfall and hope for the best.

The river grew very wide as it joined a second waterway that came from the west. The deceptively calm water rushed toward the drop-off, carrying the band of travelers with it. At the very brink of going over the edge, Buddy looked down and shouted, "Aaaaaaayyyyyyyyyy!" The waterfall was so high that Buddy didn't have enough breath to scream all the way to the bottom.

Ker-splash! The raft and all its passengers plunged into the deep pool at the base of the falls where the turbulence swirled them around and around. When they surfaced, the water was strangely calm again. Sly looked around and noticed a dock jutting out into the water. Pesky began spitting, coughing, and spitting some more as he popped his head in and out from underneath the water. Finally, he said to the others, "Hey, you guys, this water is all salty." Sly and Buddy licked their lips. Sure enough, the water was not just salty, it was extremely salty.

Sly, confused over the change, remarked to the others, "The river water was fresh. How did it turn so salty?"

Buddy was the first to figure out what happened. "We must have passed through another one of the gates of Mangonel, like the yellow one on the prairie that took me to the Fabled Forest. It looks like this one took us to another body of water. Come to think of it, Sly entered Mangonel in a similar fashion to the one we just experienced. She went over a waterfall and ended up in the River of Life. Just as she had no means of returning to where she had come from, neither do we. I think the same thing just happened to us. I think it's safe to say we have arrived in a completely different place in Mangonel."

"Hellooo!" A voice carried from the dock protruding into the shallower waters. "Are you going to swim across this large bay, or do you want a ride? I have a sturdy raft that can transport you across, for a fee."

"No thanks," said Buddy as he waded to shore. "We have had enough of rafting for one day. All we want is to know where we are so we can continue our journey east."

Disappointed, the man commented, "How am I to make any money if you don't ride my raft?" Then he brightened. "If you want to go east, you must cross this bay to the west, and it is a large bay indeed. What good fortune for you, for here I am, and I have this lovely raft that can carry you across. It will take much less time to ride than to walk."

"We thought that about the river," remarked Sly as she climbed out of the salty bay. "What would compel us to cross the bay to the west when east is in the opposite direction?

"Silly girl," said the man as he spread his arms wide. "Let me introduce myself. I am the one, the only, the remarkable, Rrrrrralph the Raftman. I am the only one with a means to cross this big, salty bay, and you simply must go to the west if you wish to travel east."

This made no sense at all to any of them, but remembering Mangonel was full of strange people, and strange things, Buddy succumbed. "Fine! How much will it cost for you to raft us to the other side, and how long will it take?"

"Oh, it will only take a few hours. If we leave now, we will be there before dark. The fare? Let me think. You are a big one, so you will cost more. Hmmmm!" Ralph puzzled over the sum for a few seconds. Then he announced, "One small gold coin, two large silver coins, and a peanut butter sandwich."

Strange dealings here in Mangonel, thought Buddy. They had plenty of money from the troll, and since there was nowhere else to get a peanut butter sandwich, Buddy could request one from the provisions bag. As he pulled the sack from his back, he looked Ralph the Raftman in the eye before he said, "Okay, it is a deal." Buddy turned his back as he reached into the bag so Ralph couldn't see what he was doing. He pulled out the coin bag to get the money to pay the fare. With a soft whisper, he asked the Merlin's bag for a peanut butter sandwich.

Turning back to Ralph, Buddy closed the bag. Stepping up to Ralph, he offered the Raftman his fee. Ralph grabbed the sandwich first. "Wow, I was sure you wouldn't have the sandwich. Without it, I could have charged more, but this is wonderful. I haven't had a peanut butter sandwich in years." Ralph immediately ate it in big gulping bites.

They all boarded the raft, and true to his word, Ralph had them across the bay before nightfall. On the opposite side,

Ralph told them to follow the path that came up to the shore. This path again was leading west. Ralph hopped back onto his raft and began paddling back to his dock. Buddy, Sly, and Pesky shrugged their shoulders at each other in a gesture of inquisitive understanding and started walking along the westerly leading path.

In time, the path turned north in a great loop. Eventually, they were going east again, just like Ralph had promised. More comfortable now that they were headed in the correct direction, they made camp for the night. The next morning, they continued their way east on the path. They followed the winding trail all day. Just as the sun began to set, they spotted a small cabin near some water. As they approached, they noticed there was a dock at the water's edge, and a raft was tied to it. It surly looked familiar. When they got close enough, they were so angry they could have stomped the ground forever. The cabin, dock, and raft all belonged to Ralph the Raftman.

They went to the cabin door and banged on it until Ralph opened it. "Nice to see you all again," he said cheerily.

Sly was ready to bite him on the leg, but she didn't. Instead she growled, "Why did you take us on that raft and send us on a full day's journey along that silly path? All it did was lead us right back to you. We could have just gone on our way from here and been that much closer to our destination."

"First, young lady, like I told you, you must go west so you can go east. If you are not someplace west of here, how can you possibly go east? Everyone who comes here has only three directions to travel. South, to the Great Salt Ocean, but nobody really wants to go there. North, but in order to go north I send travelers to the south to the ocean, just a short way in that direction," he said, and he pointed south. "In this way, they are able to start their northerly journey from the south. Then there is east and west, which in either case they cross this bay. You see, it is relatively simple."

"No use arguing," declared Pesky, "we are getting nowhere standing here talking to Ralph about what is already done. Let's move on." While Sly was talking to Ralph, Pesky had snuck down to the raft and untied the ropes that fastened it to the dock. The raft would drift about and come to shore again someplace on the bay, but it would serve Ralph right for having delayed them and charging them for the privilege.

With their belongings in hand, Buddy, Sly, and Pesky gazed at the easterly path. With a grin of satisfaction, they planted their first steps into their next adventure in the kingdom of Mangonel.

Dictionary—Chapter 12

Brink: *The very edge of something*

Brightened: *To become enthusiastic, lively, or happy*

Churning: *To move violently about*

Compelled: *Forced to do something*

Conceded: *Admit defeat or give up*

Creek: *A stream that eventually flows into a river*

Cruise: *To travel at an easy pace*

Current: *A steady flow of water or air in one direction*

Declare: *To state something in an open and emphatic way*

Disappointed: *Unhappy because something did not turn out the way it was expected*

Dock: *An area of water adjacent to a pier*

Emerge: *To appear out from behind something*

Fashion: *A particular way of behaving or doing something*

Flexible: *Able to bend or be bent repeatedly without damage or injury*

Gazed: *Look for a long time without distraction*

Improved: *In a better or more valuable condition*

Jabber: *To talk or say something rapidly and excitedly*

Jut: *To stick out*

Mischievous: *Behaving in a naughty but fun, not serious way*

Nightfall: *The beginning of night*

Obstructions: *Something that causes or forms a blockage, interference*

Opposite: *Pointing, facing, moving, or doing something in complete contrast*

Overboard: *Over the side of a ship, boat, or any watercraft and into the water*

Plunged: *To move suddenly downward or forward*

Pondered: *To think about something carefully and over a long period of time*

Precious: *Highly valued and much loved*

Privilege: *An advantage or benefit that is not available to everyone*

Rapids: *A part of a riverbed where the water moves very fast, usually over rocks*

Realized: *To know, understand, and accept something*

Recovered: *To get back something that had been previously lost*

Relatively: *Comparatively*

Request: *To ask for something in a formal way*

Scampered: *To run quickly or playfully*

Shoreline: *The land where a body of water meets the shore*

Signaled: *A bit of information communicated by a gesture or sign*

Turbulence: *A state of confusion caused by unpredictable changes*

CHAPTER 13

Oh, So Tipsy

Having been misguided by Ralph the Raftman, but once again heading east, Buddy and his friends continued their journey toward the next town. It was a pleasant walk, and thankfully, a short one. There were no obstacles to cross, there were no unforeseen encounters with strange people, and there were no surprises in the weather. In all, it was just a nice stroll through the park-like forest.

It only took a few hours to get from the previous night's campsite to the edge of the next town. This place looked very strange. All the buildings, fences, and other objects were built at a slant. In order to view the town correctly from where they stood, they had to tilt their heads to the right. When they did, everything looked the way it should, vertical, but then the ground was at a slant. It was a mystery. Buddy asked no one in particular, "What would have caused these people to build their town in such a manner?"

In the past, their anticipation of seeing people, eating some food, and finding a place to rest would have them nearly running into any village or town they came across. Now, these three had become savvy travelers. Each one, Buddy, Sly, and Pesky, found a stone they could use as a chair. They sat down to gaze at the town while they pondered what to do next. Before they were going to go headlong into some new predicament, they decided to discuss what they might be facing, what they would do in case something went wrong, and what other options they had. After all they had been through, they knew that experience is sometimes a hard way to learn. Fortunately, their many adventures in Mangonel had taught Buddy and his friends patience and perseverance. Buddy, Sly, and Pesky, without anyone else to rely on, had to learn nearly everything the hard way. Any new lesson learned was shared so no one would make the same mistake.

Pesky, ready to let his stomach lead the way, spoke first. "I'm hungry. I can smell fish cooking over there in that town, and that smell isn't helping matters much. I say we go over and investigate where the aroma is coming from. If they have extra, we can ask if they will give us some."

At first Sly and Buddy ignored his remarks, and his suggestion. Sly, with a look of concentration, softly added, "The way people build something is no reason to cause suspicion. It could be they fashioned the town in this manner because …" Her voice trailed off, and then, after a pause she said, "I can't think of a single reason, but I am positively certain they have one."

Buddy thought they may have done this because everyone had bent necks, or maybe one eye was higher than the other. Neither Sly nor Pesky thought these could be the reasons. To be kind, they shrugged their shoulders in a gesture of "Who knows?" Then again, who could guess what people do or why they do it, especially in Mangonel? Everything here seemed to be as strange as could be.

They all sat and thought some more. Suddenly, without another word, Buddy stood, and as he hefted the provisions bag over his shoulder, he looked at the town and started walking. With a tone of final determination, he declared, "We'll never know if we don't go ask. Besides, Pesky's talk about food has made me hungry too."

The others rose and followed behind Buddy as he headed for the town. The first thing they noticed was that all the people walked upright, and nobody had crooked necks or one eye higher than the other. The whole town was on a slant, but the people were vertical. The three friends stopped and shook their heads in disbelief.

When they entered the town, everyone they encountered began to follow them. About halfway into the town, they arrived at a fountain. To one side of the fountain was a post with a bulletin board attached. A group of people were gathered about reading an announcement that had been pinned to the board. Neither Sly nor Pesky were strong enough to push their way to the front. Buddy picked up his two friends in one strong arm and made his way to the sign. Sly read the posting:

"Any perpetrator pilfering a possession of another person shall be prosecuted and punished posthaste." The notice was signed: *"This proclamation presented by Peter Poppernoch, presiding president."*

"Now what in the world do you suppose that means?" asked Buddy.

Someone in the crowd had heard Buddy's comment. He spoke up. "The president is upset about the theft that took place yesterday. He's warning everyone that he will not stand for it, and anyone who steals will be severely punished."

Buddy and Sly couldn't help but glance at Pesky. They knew he didn't take anything yesterday. He was with them on their way here. Then everyone noticed the three strangers in their midst.

"Hey!" called out one man. "Who are you?"

Another shouted, "Where did you come from?"

A woman almost screamed in excitement, "What do you want?"

Without thinking, Pesky addressed the woman's question by shouting at the top of his lungs, *"Food!"* Somehow that silly, unexpected answer broke all the tension. Everyone started to relax at that moment. Some were even giggling behind their hands. Then the president arrived. "Please provide me with a proper explanation of what progress my posting has prompted." *Evidently the mayor has an obsession with using words with the letter* p, thought Sly.

"We were reading your announcement when these three strangers arrived, Mr. President Poppernoch," stated a young man in the group.

"Perfect, I will not pose a pretense pertaining to whom these new pedestrians might be, but I will promptly procure a proper identification," puffed the president. "So," the president said as he turned to address Buddy, Sly, and Pesky, "please provide me with your names and a pronouncement of purpose for your presence." Then looking at the masked raccoon, he added accusingly, "Perhaps you have some proposal pertaining to the perpetrator who performed yesterday's pilfering."

Buddy couldn't control himself. With a soft roar in his voice, he addressed the mayor. "Enough with all the *p* words. I also suggest you not cast blame before you are certain of the facts." Calmer, he offered a bit of his story about how he came to Mangonel and met his new friends and how they were looking to go east to find a way back home. While Buddy spoke, Peter, the president, and all the people nodded their heads, indicating that they understood. Nobody interrupted. Buddy then asked his questions. "What town is this? How much farther can we go to the east, and why are all your buildings slanted?"

This was quickly followed by Pesky chiming in, "Don't forget to ask if we can get something to eat."

"Sorry," said Peter, "I just love the letter *p*. I use it whenever I can. Sometimes it becomes annoying to others." All the townspeople were nodding again. "You are in the town of Tipsy. This town began when a few people from the mountains on earth found their way into Mangonel. Their mountainous terrain forced them to build their homes on sort of a slant to accommodate the tilted ground. You see, they were so accustomed to tilting houses, when they arrived here they just didn't know how to build things straight. The result is this town, which sort of tips to one side."

"Interesting," remarked Buddy. A quizzical look came over Peter's face as he told them east was only a short distance over the nearby knoll. "Why go east when there is so much more land north and west?" he asked. "You cannot go much further east because you will run out of land. The Great Salt Ocean is only a mile or two in that direction," he said as he pointed east.

Buddy looked relieved. He glanced in Sly's direction. "Finally, we have gone as far east as we can go. Now we can begin our search in the west." Sly ruined this thought when she explained that they were also all the way south in Mangonel as well as all the way east. "Mind you," she stated, "We still have the entire east side of Mangonel to search as well, from here all the way to the northerly border."

"Oh, yes," said Peter. "There is still plenty of land north of here, and when you go further north, the land goes east some more, until you pass the Pointing Inlet; then you must travel along the westerly side of the bay formed by the peninsula. There is still more land north of the peninsula, but do not go so far north that you cross the border into the Forbidden Land."

"Why not?" asked Pesky.

"Because it is forbidden," warned the president, scornfully looking at the raccoon.

With all the questions asked, and everyone satisfied with the answers given, the townspeople asked if the travelers wished to stay for dinner. Pesky was thrilled. He asked if they were having fish, his favorite food. The townspeople explained that fish is almost all they ever ate. They lived so close to the ocean that they went fishing all the time. The fishermen brought their catches to the fountain at the center plaza, where it was distributed to the cooks, who prepared it for the entire town.

The travelers were taken to one of the many tables that rested on a slanted platform. Each table had enough chairs to sit about fifty people. Everyone began sitting down to a feast laid out on the tables before them. The only problem they had was that all the plates, glasses, and silverware had to be set in notched-out spaces cut into the table tops or they would slide off. To assist in adjusting for the slant, all the plates, cups, and bowls had one side taller than the other, so the food would stay on the plates, in the bowls, and in their glasses. Sly thought all this was more trouble than what it was worth. Buddy agreed completely. Pesky was too involved with his meal to even notice there was a problem.

As people finished eating their meals, they got up from the table to serve those who were doing the serving. This way, everyone got a good meal, and the same people were not always assigned to serving. The rotation worked wonderfully in this small town. Then, one of the new servers stopped dead in his tracks. He stared at Buddy's bag. It took a little while for him to recognize what he was looking at, but eventually he did see it for what it was. "Wait just a second," he said aloud. "Our guests here are eating our food while they march around with a super sack. They should be feeding us. Everything in the world is in that sack—enough for all of us." Before Buddy could figure out what the fellow was talking about, the server grabbed for the sack. Pesky, having once been a thief of sorts, was very quick. He was off his chair and reached the sack just ahead of the man. Pesky started running toward the edge of town before the server could react. He ran as fast as he could. The little raccoon had saved the day with his quick reflexes and even faster getaway.

Everyone at the table glared at Buddy and Sly. "Why wouldn't you share with us? We are sharing with you." The town was growing angry. Someone in the group shouted, "If they stole that bag, which is likely, because nobody has those anymore, then that would be a perfect place to hide Wanda's missing broom." Before things got worse, Buddy rose to his full height, which by now was fearsome. He looked over the angry crowd, let out a growl, and loudly advised Sly, "Let's be on our way before I eat one of these nice people instead of the fish," though he never would. That frightened the Tipsy Town people enough that Buddy and Sly could make their way to the edge of town to meet Pesky. Then they ran from the place as fast as their feet could carry them.

When they stopped to rest, they were far, far away from Tipsy. Sly was thinking about what had happened, like she always did. "Buddy," she began, "People are so greedy. I think I know why there are so few provision bags and why this may be the last. Whenever someone was in possession of one of these magic bags, they probably emptied them through misuse. Remember the warning Mable gave us? She cautioned that if we take what we don't need, or what we can get for ourselves, then that item would be removed from the bag forever." Then she looked to find Pesky. When she spotted him, she gratefully said, "Thank you, Pesky, for being so alert. You saved our most precious possession."

Pesky was embarrassed from the compliment. He wasn't used to this sort of praise. He was just happy to have good friends like Sly and Buddy.

Suddenly the raccoon perked up even more. Another good idea had just popped into his head. "If the Tipsy people recognized the bag, there will be others who will see the bag for what it is. Maybe we should disguise it somehow."

"Magnificent idea!" exclaimed Sly. They all began discussing how to best hide the sack. They tossed all manner of suggestions for disguising the bag as they walked east toward the beach of the Great Salt Ocean, where they would soon turn to the north on their continuing quest to find a way home.

Dictionary—Chapter 13

Accommodate: *To allow for something without conflict*

Accusingly: *Blaming, suggesting somebody has done something wrong*

Accustomed: *To become familiar with something or someone*

Adjust: *To change something slightly*

Alert: *Watchful and ready to deal with whatever happens*

Compliment: *Something said to express praise or approval*

Concentration: *To focus the mind on one specific thought, task, topic, idea, or subject*

Determination: *With a fixed purpose and firmness of will or intention*

Disbelief: *Thinking something is not true or someone is not truthful*

Disguise: *To change something so it cannot be recognized*

Distributed: *To be passed out in equal or near-equal proportions*

Embarrassed: *Painfully self-conscious and ill at ease*

Encounter: *To come up against something difficult*

Fearsome: *To create fear*

Grasp: *To understand something's meaning*

Headlong: *Moving forward fast and out of control*

Heft: *To lift something up, especially with a burst of energy*

Ignore: *Refuse to notice or give attention to*

Inlet: *A narrow opening in a coastline*

Interrupted: *To speak out of turn while someone else is already speaking*

Investigate: *Look at something very carefully to obtain an explanation*

Magnificent: *Wonderful, superb, outstanding*

Misdirected: *To give someone wrong directions or instructions*

Obsession: *An idea or feeling that completely occupies the mind*

Options: *Choices*

Pedestrians: *People who are traveling on foot*

Peninsula: *A narrow piece of land that juts out from the mainland into the water*

Perk: *An increase in happiness*

Perpetrator: *The person who commits a crime*

Perseverance: *Steady and continued action, patience, persistence*

Pertaining: *To have a connection with something*

Pilfering: *Stealing of small things*

Ponder: *To consider carefully*

Pose: *To present something*

Posting: *A written announcement*

Posthaste: *Right away*

Predicament: *A difficult situation*

Presence: *Being in the same area*

Present: *To give or hand something to someone*

Presiding: *Officially in charge*

Pretense: *A way of behaving that is not truthful or genuine*

Proclamation: *A public announcement*

Procure: *To get something*

Prompted: *Caused someone to act*

Proposal: *A suggestion*

Prosecute: *Legal action against someone*

Quizzical: *Questioning, puzzlement*

Reflexes: *How fast someone reacts to something, usually automatically*

Relieve: *To end or lessen something to give a temporary break*

Rotation: *Turning motion like that of a wheel*

Savvy: *Shrewd, practical, wise in judgment*

Scornful: *Feeling of great dislike*

Slant: *To be at an angle or to set something at an angle*

Stare: *Look directly at somebody or something for a long time without moving*

Suspicion: *A belief that something is true but with no way to prove it*

Tension: *An uneasy feeling that makes it difficult to relax*

Thrilled: *To feel intense excitement, feel great pleasure*

Tilted: *To place something at a slope or slant*

Troublesome: *Causing difficulties*

Unforeseen: *Not expected*

Vertical: *Straight up and down*

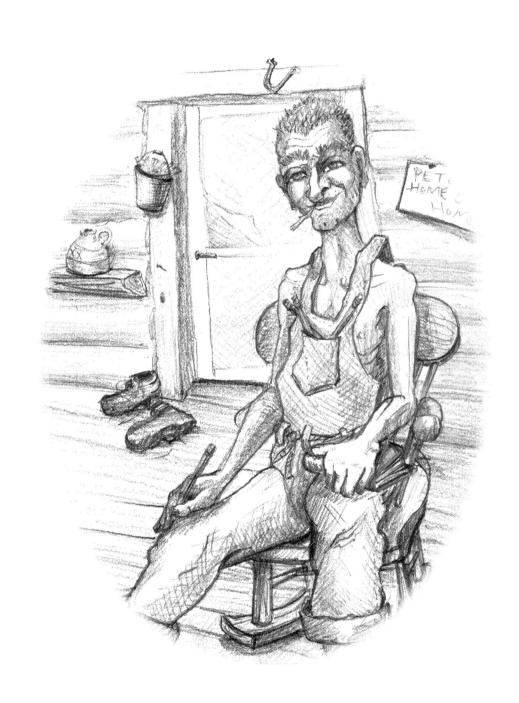

CHAPTER 14

Meetin' Pete

Barely escaping the town of Tipsy, and the town's greedy desire to take their provisions bag, Buddy, Sly, and Pesky were eventually able to stroll along a nice little road to the beach of the Great Salt Ocean. Upon arrival at the beach, they gazed upon the wide body of water that stretched beyond their view north, south, and east. None of them had ever seen an ocean. It was immense. They couldn't believe its size or the amount of water, but the water was salty, so they had no use for it.

Buddy recalled Ryla's map showing another ocean to the south. Their conversation with Ralph the Raftman confirmed this information, so they turned left to face north. This was the direction they would travel to continue their search for a way home, at least for a while. They wanted to finish probing the eastern regions of the kingdom of Mangonel before venturing west again.

Prior to setting off into their next adventure, Pesky reminded them that they needed to disguise their provisions bag to keep prying eyes and hands away from it. They tried everything. They smeared it with mud. They rubbed it in the grass. They jumped up and down on it. They attached straps to make it look different. Nothing they tried changed it enough. To make matters worse, as soon as they finished messing it up, it cleaned itself up to look good as new.

Pesky, the crafty one, came up with an idea, "Buddy carries the bag over his shoulder, right? It's out in the open all the time, for everyone to see, right? If we were to create a diversion to make it appear to be something similar, yet different, nobody would suspect it for what it really is."

Sly stared at the raccoon in astonishment. "And what do you suppose we have been doing for the past few hours, Mr. Raccoon?" she asked.

"Let's make it look like a hobo's sack," offered Pesky.

Buddy had no idea what a hobo's sack was, so Sly explained. "A hobo is someone who has very few belongings. He carries all he owns with him wherever he goes by wrapping his things in a cloth and tying the corners together. Then he ties that to a stick. While traveling he puts the stick over his shoulder for easy toting."

Just a piece of cloth would be too small to use for the provisions bag. Besides, they had no cloth to use. Pesky was sitting closest to the bag. The next thing Sly and Buddy knew, the raccoon was holding a large blanket, just the right size to bundle the provisions bag. "Where did you get that?" asked Buddy. Then he knew. It came from the provisions bag.

Pesky looked sheepish, but he defended what he had done. "We can take from the bag what we cannot get by ourselves, correct? I don't see any place where we can get a blanket, do you? I asked the provisions bag for a blanket to hide the bag in, and this blanket was inside for us to use. We can get a stick from the ground almost anywhere in Mangonel, so I didn't ask for one of those."

Once the others heard Pesky's explanation, they agreed his was a good idea. Buddy tied the provisions bag in the blanket, which was the perfect size, while Sly searched for a sturdy stick. Once completed, Buddy confirmed that the provisions bag certainly looked like a sack that Sly had described. With the bag properly hidden from curious eyes, they began heading north.

The three companions walked along the beach for a long time. Eventually, they came across another river that was draining into the ocean. Buddy tried to remember the map Ryla had etched into the cave dirt. His memory was excellent, but the map was fading into the past. The details were escaping him. If he was correct, the river before them was part of the River River, and was called the South River River. All the river and mountain names in Mangonel were too confusing. *Everyone in Mangonel should own a map*, thought Buddy. After crossing this river, they would have to cross another as they went north. That river was yet another branch of the River River as it traveled east from the waterfall from which they had fallen. When they reached that point of crossing, they could turn east once more to try to find the Pointing Inlet. If the president of Tipsy was correct, their easterly search might be at an end, or they might find a way out of Mangonel.

Crossing this South River River wasn't difficult, but it was an event to remember. Buddy, who was the largest, waded into the flowing river to see how deep it was. Just a few steps into the water, the bottom fell off at a drastic rate. Down he went. Buddy began to move his feet to stay afloat as he tried to reach the shore. Surprisingly, he found he could swim. Instead of getting out of the water right away, he swam around, testing his new skill. He discovered not only could he swim, but he was pretty good at it. It struck him funny that there were so many things he could do if he just tried.

When Buddy got out of the water, he was all smiles. "Hey you two, did you see that? I can swim!" he exclaimed. "This river is wide, but it doesn't look like it is flowing very fast. Why don't you guys climb onto my back? I'll swim us to the other side," he suggested. Sly and Pesky were glad to stay out of the water. They scampered up onto Buddy's broad back. The big bear carefully entered the water so he wouldn't knock the others off. When they were settled, he began paddling his way to the other side of the river. Shortly after entering the water, Pesky became frightened. The raccoon dug his claws into Buddy's back to hold on tighter.

"Ouch!" shouted Buddy. Pesky eased up on his grip but only a little. Buddy swam as fast as he could because Pesky's claws were sharp, and they hurt.

On the other side of the South River River, they headed east once more. Very soon, they spotted a worn down, shabby house. There was smoke coming from the chimney, which told them someone was home. When the group got nearer, they could see a man in a rocking chair sitting on the porch. He had a pad of paper in one hand and a pencil in the other. The man was tall, almost as tall as Buddy, but was nearly as thin as his pencil. With no effort at all, the man was turning his pencil in circles, twirling it in and out of his fingers. He never dropped it but kept turning it round and round.

The guy stopped rocking, took a small stick he had been chewing on from his mouth, and stared at the new arrivals. "My, my, my! What have we he-a?" he asked with a Southern drawl.

Sly answered his question with a question. "And we might inquire in like manner in regard to whom we are speaking."

"Fine, I'll answer first. I'm Pete. Some calls me Pencil-Packin' Pete. This he-a is my home. Nobody else is he-a but me, and there ain't no neighbors, so thar's no need to be a fearin' me. Y'all are safe," said Pete. "Come closer, set your buns upon the steps, ifin you like, and tells me who y'all might be."

Again Sly spoke for the group. She told Pete a shortened version of who they were, as well as where they were going.

She finished by asking, "Why are you all alone? What do you do here all day and night?"

Pete replied, "Land-O-Goshen child, I sleeps at night, just like most people. Durin' the day, I writes me whatever I feels like puttin' down on paper. Right now thar ain't nuttin' I wants to write, so I just sits he-a an' rock in my thinkin' char. As fo why I's all alone, seems nobody likes me, cause when I gets to writin', stuff starts ta happen. That's when they all gets up an' leaves. Ya see, what I writes down comes true. Watch, I kin show y'all." Pete put the stick back in his mouth, held the pencil so he could write with it, scratched his head with the eraser, and said. "Sposin' I wants a tree right thar about ten feet from this he-a house. I just writes it down, like this." Pete wrote some words, and when the group turned around, sure enough, there was a tree standing just about ten feet from where the porch ended.

Buddy walked over and scratched his back against it to make sure it was real. I was real all right. "Seems kind of handy to me," he said.

"Sure nuff, 'cept thar ain't nobody likes it when I gets to scrachtin' down a bunch o' stuff. Then they all gets all jittery-like an' pack up. Next day theys all gone away without nary a word. Not much use in that, wouldn't ya say?"

A moment of silence passed before the ever-hungry Pesky spoke up. "Say, Mr. Pete, you think you could write something about a nice cooked meal, with plenty of fish, rice, bread, and vegetables?"

"What a rip-roarin' idée that is, young man," remarked Pete. He began writing very fast. As the group watched, a large table appeared in the yard under the new tree. Then came a large tray filled with fish, a tray of roasted pork, a big bowl of beef stew, roasted chickens, baked turkey, a huge bowl of hot rice, a platter full of bread and butter, bowls of green beans, corn, asparagus, broccoli, several pitchers of water, glasses and plates, and utensils and napkins for everyone.

"Where does all this come from?" asked Sly.

"Don't rightly know, ma'am. I just does the writin'."

After they were all stuffed, Pencil-Packin' Pete did some more writing, and the table, chairs, and food all disappeared. By this time it was dark. Pete scribbled some more on his pad, and a large tent filled the place where the table and food had once been. Inside the tent were cots, blankets, and pillows. "This guy could take the place of the Merlin's Bag," whispered Pesky.

Sly, who had been deep in thought, mumbled under her breath, "Do you suppose he could write something to send each of us home?"

They all went to sleep with that thought in mind, each dreaming of home.

The next morning Pete had a big breakfast all prepared for them. A new table and chairs set sat next to the tent. Food was piled high with all manner of breakfast fare. There was an array of cereals, milk, doughnuts, eggs, sausage, hot chocolate, pancakes, waffles, fruit, and so much more. When they were just about finished eating, Buddy asked Pete if he could write something on his pad to send him and his friends back to their homes on earth.

Pete frowned. "Sorry, son, kain't do that. I did that oncet. The people didn't go no place. They just stood thar a-starin' at me. Then they got all angry cause I didn't send them on to their home. I ain't got nuttin' to do with it. I just writes it. I figure the only reason they didn't go anywhere was 'cause they now had a new home here in Mangonel. Best I kin do fer ya is to write down where ya wants to go in the kingdom. Let me know where, and I'll do that fer y'all."

"We better think on this before we make our request," Sly explained to her friends. "You see, if we say something about going east, Pete might just send us to the opposite end of the ocean. If we say we are seeking to go to the next town north, we might skip right over the gate that could take us home. This is a difficult decision to make and a dangerous one."

Pesky was still eating. All the talk of home made him think about his own mother. He tried to say out loud that he wanted to go to his endearing mother. His mouth was still full of food, so his words came out all distorted. "Thened us to my endearin' mompth," he slurred.

From all his practice, Pencil-Packin' Pete could write very fast. Before Buddy or Sly could stop him, he had already written what he heard. "Don' know why anyone would wanna go thar, but so be it. To the Never-Endin' Swamp it is."

In a flash Buddy, Sly, and Pesky, still with his mouth full, found themselves ankle deep in a dreary, gray swamp land that smelled bad.

Buddy and Sly glared at Pesky. "Sometimes you are more trouble than you are worth," hissed Buddy. "Go find your own way. I have had about all I can take. Don't we have enough trouble without you stirring up more? Go find someone else to pester."

Had it not been for Sly reminding Buddy how Pesky had saved the provisions bag, and had helped disguise their most valuable possession, Pesky might have been cast out.

"Okay," groaned Buddy, "you can stay. From now on be very careful of what you do and what you say." Looking about, seeing no sun, having no bearings, and not knowing where they were, Buddy sighed. "What do we do now? Which way should we go?"

Pesky closed his eyes. He spun around in a circle several times. When he stopped spinning, he almost fell down. He steadied himself, and pointed in front of him. When he opened his eyes, he said, "That way seems as good as any."

Buddy looked at Sly; without so much as a word, he turned around and headed in just the opposite direction from where Pesky was pointing.

Dictionary—Chapter 14

Astonishment: *Great amazement*

Certainly: *Without any doubt*

Chimney: *A structure to allow the venting of gas or smoke*

Confirmed: *Having been found to be true*

Curious: *Eager to know something*

Defended: *Protected*

Desire: *To want something*

Distorted: *In an altered state, to give an inaccurate report of something*

Diversion: *Something that takes someone's attention away from something else*

Drastic: *Having a powerful effect*

Dreary: *Gloomy*

Ease: *To remove a measure of difficulty*

Endearing: *Loved and lovable*

Escaping: *Breaking free from captivity, to avoid something unpleasant*

Etched: *Carved*

Eventually: *The end, especially after experiencing many problems or setbacks*

Fading: *Gradually becoming less bright*

Glared: *Stared sternly*

Hobo: *A poor and homeless person, especially one who travels around*

Immense: *Very large*

Inquire: *Ask*

Mutter: *To say something quietly*

Probing: *Investigating*

Prying: *Inquisitive, snooping into someone's private affairs*

Regard: *To be about somebody or something*

Shabby: *Worn out, frayed*

Sheepish: *Timid, showing meekness*

Similar: *Sharing some qualities but not identical*

Slur: *To speak indistinctively,*

Stroll: *Walk unhurriedly*

Surprisingly: *To make somebody amazed*

Toting: *Carrying something*

Utensil: *A tool or container, especially those used in the kitchen*

Venturing: *To do something with a bit of danger involved*

CHAPTER 15

The Never-Ending Swamp

Buddy and his companions were inadvertently swept from Pencil-Packin' Pete's cabin and deposited in the middle of the Never-Ending Swamp. The swamp was nasty. The mud smelled terrible and was ankle deep under the nearly black water. The sky was covered in a foggy mist created by the dampness of the swamp, the heat of the day, and the coolness of the air above the trees. The gray, cloudlike covering never lifted, day or night. The sun was very difficult to see through the dense fog hanging low overhead. At night, the moon and stars were nonexistent. This was a hot, sticky, wet, stinking, bug-filled place none of them liked.

The swamp proved to live up to its name. Buddy and his group marked a trail as best they could as they traveled. Every day they walked until it got dark. Day after day after day, they went. Each morning they would check their last few markings to put themselves on the correct path. Sly would retreat to the nearest marking, while Buddy would go back two markings. They lined themselves up in a straight line, and then they directed Pesky to a position up ahead. They should have hop-scotched their way in this manner until they exited the swamp, but they had not thought of it. Lining themselves up each morning, they were at least able to start the day in the same direction they had left off the night before. After getting settled on which way to go, and packing up all their belongings, they began each morning just like the one before.

One particular day Sly noticed a mark on one of the trees, but it wasn't one of theirs. The mark was obviously put there for the same purpose they were making navigational markings. Others who were in this swamp, or had been, had tried to find their way out, just like Buddy, Sly and Pesky were doing. On closer inspection they could see that the gouge in the tree was well healed. The passerby had been through this area a long, long time ago. All three travelers had the same thought. *Did this traveler find his way out of this swamp? Maybe his trail blazing could help us escape.* But none dared say it.

Instead, Buddy asked the others, "Do you think anybody else is still around?" Neither Pesky nor Sly answered. They were more worried that the person, or persons, who made the marks in this horrible place might not be friendly.

By the end of that day, they were extremely tired. As they were about to set up camp, Pesky spotted something up ahead resting against an exposed tree root. There, propped up in a notch formed by the roots, was the skeleton of a man. His clothes had all rotted away. There was nothing left of his garments but strips of cloth draped over some of the bones.

The top of his hat had torn through, and the brim rested over his shoulders like a silly bib. His right arm was nestled on a root that held one hand out of the water. The skeletal man tightly clenched a rolled-up piece of tree bark in his boney hand. Sly moved very cautiously toward the skeleton. Standing beside the bones, she took hold of the hand holding the rolled bark. She had to work at the man's fingers to pry it loose, but in time she got it free. She carefully unrolled the brittle bark and found a warning written on it. Very slowly, quietly, as if in reverence to the poor man who wrote it, she read what was written. The script announced, *"Be very careful or you will go in circles. I discovered too late that the way out is marked in moss."*

"Now what do you suppose that means?" pondered Pesky.

Together Sly and Buddy said, "I'm not sure." Then Buddy suggested it might be a riddle. There was a clue in the warning. The key to getting out of the swamp was given to them. They just had to figure out how to use it.

While in the Never-Ending Swamp, the provisions bag came in very handy. If they didn't have the magical bag with them, they too might have died, maybe even before they could have reached the man with the note of warning. Without it, they would not have been able to get anything they needed. There was no food, no dry spots to get out of the muck, no shelter, no blankets. Nothing. Each night they would reach into the bag and pull out some dry planks. They would rest the planks across some exposed roots that stuck up out of the water so they could make their beds in a high and dry place. They would then get some blankets, and a large piece of canvas to use as a roof over their beds. When everything was settled, they would reach in the bag for something to eat. Survival would have been impossible without the provisions bag. Every morning, they packed up all they had taken from the bag and replaced what they had not used.

None of them wanted to stay too near the skeleton, but none of them wanted to leave until they figured out the clue. If they left this place, they might leave the clue behind, so they made camp. They stayed at this unpleasant location for two full days while they contemplated the message. What could it mean? "Marked in moss," was what it said. They examined every bit of moss in the area, over and over again, but there were no hidden marks, nothing out of the ordinary. It was just moss growing on the trees.

On the third day, Sly finally figured out the clue while searching in the area where the skeleton man rested. She decided that the moss itself had to be the clue, and so she paid close attention to it as she walked around many, many trees. No matter where she went, she noticed the moss grew on the same side of every tree, or nearly so.

There was no mark in the moss, like they all thought. Sly ran back to the others. "I think I solved the puzzle," she excitedly declared, and then she explained her discovery to them. "You see, the moss is the mark we are searching for. All the trees have moss on them, and the moss is almost always on the same side of every tree. If we keep following the moss we will not veer too far right or left. We won't go in circles. By keeping a close eye on the moss, we will head in basically the same direction all day long. As long as we can see the moss, we could conceivably travel at night, if we chose to do so. With the moss as our guide, we will eventually find our way out of this dreadful place."

Five more days passed as they traveled in the murky, depressing swamp. Finally, they came upon a lip outlining some higher ground. They were traveling side by side at this point, and they all simultaneously placed a foot up onto dry land. They heaved themselves up onto the ledge and into a dense fog. Here, finally on dry land, there were no trees to guide their way. Holding each other's hands, together they took another step forward. At their back feet, the fog was as thick as soup, but the sun was shining brightly on their faces all the way down to their front feet. It was like walking out of a dark room into a bright sunny day. The fog at the end of the swamp was like a wall. They were all so happy they began whooping and dancing in circles. Oh happy days! They were out of the swamp. They had made it.

Suddenly, Buddy stopped dancing and pointed out into the flat prairie. "Hhhhhey you guys," he stuttered. "Look at that. What in the kingdom of Mangonel is that?" Buddy was staring at a tall, glistening pole, or at least it looked like a pole from where they stood.

Approaching carefully, they began examining the object while walking around it in a wide circle. This object wasn't a pole at all. They were staring at a large slab of flat rock standing on one edge. The flat stone faces were polished to a high shine that reflected the sunlight like a mirror. The slab was a perfect rectangle with a height of about twenty feet, a width of about eight feet, and was about twelve inches thick. They moved nearer until they were so close they could reach out and touch the surface if they wanted.

Buddy's curiosity got the better of him. He rubbed his paw up and down the middle of the odd stone. It was as smooth as it looked. He then began to run his paw horizontally around the stone until, to his surprise, he felt the stone move. He instinctively jumped back. Touching the stone once more, but closer toward an edge, he was able to make the stone swing freely. Amazed at how smoothly it moved, he gave it a mighty shove. This sent the slab spinning on a center fulcrum. Its spinning was similar to a revolving door at a store. As it spun, Buddy was able to see a completely different terrain when the door was 90 degrees from its original position. When the stone stopped, it stopped in the same place as it was when they arrived.

Buddy could barely speak, but still managed to utter, "Amazing! I believe this is another gate, sort of like the yellow one I came across in the field outside of the Land of Helpers. When the stone was spinning, I could see what is on the other side. This passage will put me somewhere high in a mountain range."

Sly could see where this was going. Immediately she demanded, "We will all go together."

"No," said Buddy, "It may be dangerous. I am the largest and the strongest. I should go first. If it's safe, I'll come back to get you."

Pesky was frightened. "What happens if you can't come back?" he asked. "I think we should all go together, no matter what is on the other side."

Buddy thought this over and then came up with this solution. "I'll go through first. Then I'll come right back. If I can't come back, we'll know right away. At that point you can decide to follow if you like or not. If I do come back, we can make up our minds regarding our next steps and what our best choice of action will be. Right now, I say you need to let me go alone to see what we will be getting ourselves into."

Sly agreed this was a good plan. Pesky was still afraid. His agreement was tinged with a smidgen of reluctance.

With everyone in accord, Buddy gingerly pushed the stone on one edge and walked slowly with the door as it spun. Soon he was gone. The door kept spinning. As it swung around, Buddy came around with it. "Hi guys!" he said as they came into view. "I didn't let go of the stone that time, so I'll go once more. This time I'll walk away from the gate a little before I try to come back." Off he went on his second journey to the other side.

It took a minute or two before Buddy came back with a big grin on his face. "We have found a gate home. I'm sure of it. I think it goes to the same mountains where I was born. I'm finally going home." The others looked sad until Buddy offered to take them along. "Why not go home with me?" he said. "Once we get to my house we can figure out what to do next."

Sly and Pesky took several deep breaths before they went through the gate. Once on the other side, they took in the landscape. Sure enough, there were mountains, large mountains. The group had arrived about half way up one side of this mountain range. Buddy's home was only a short distance from here; he could feel it. He began walking up the steep slope with the others not far behind. Experience and habits formed in Mangonel had Buddy marking trees and rocks as they traveled. In this way, should he be wrong, and this not be Colorado, they could find their way back to the stone gate.

After hiking for a few hours, they came to a place where they were able to see the city. As a bear, Buddy knew he couldn't just stroll into a place full of people. They would capture him and carry him away. This was something he hadn't thought of when he was wishing to be a bear. Crestfallen, he explained to the others, "We are home, on earth, but home is not going to be the same for me." He held back the tears and choked back the crying that threatened to overcome him. Mumbling to himself, he said in a sad voice, "I guess as long as I am Buddy Bear and not Buddy Bailey, I will never see my mother again."

Sly gently placed a paw on his shoulder. Seeing Buddy in tears, Pesky wasn't sure what to do. Without warning, Sly called out in a cheerful voice, "Let's do some exploring. Maybe we can find an answer to our problems if we search for it."

No one moved for a minute or two. They were waiting for Buddy while he stared down at the area he used to call home. Having finally made up his mind, he shook his shoulders, turned away from the town, smiled at his friends, and even though his tone showed his disappointment, he announced, "What are we waiting for?"

Dictionary—Chapter 15

Accord: *In agreement*

Brim: *To be fully at the top or at the very edge*

Clenched: *To hold or grip something tightly*

Constantly: *Ever present, happening, or done repeatedly*

Crestfallen: *Disappointed*

Deposited: *To put something somewhere*

Extremely: *To a very high degree*

Fulcrum: *The point at which a lever turns*

Gingerly: *Very cautiously*

Gouge: *To carve out a hole or groove*

Heaved: *Lifted with much effort*

Hop-scotch: *A game wherein the players move about a set course on one foot*

Horizontally: *Stretching left to right, parallel with the horizon*

Inadvertently: *Without intention*

Landscape: *A section of scenery of some particular type*

Nasty: *Generally unpleasant or disagreeable*

Nonexistent: *Does not exist, not real*

Particular: *One item or person chosen out of several*

Script: *Written words*

Smidgen: *A small amount*

Tinged: *Touched*

Veer: *To swerve*

CHAPTER 16

Home Is in the Heart

Colorado, Buddy's home, was not at all what he expected. The mountains were high and difficult to navigate. The city was a scary place. He knew from experience as a boy what people did to bears who wandered into such places. He was on earth, but he wasn't home. He felt a sadness he had never known before. It was all very disappointing.

Sly and Pesky could see Buddy was upset, so they kept their distance. They remained very quiet while they waited for Buddy to adjust to his new problem. As they waited for him, they searched for animal tracks to see if other bears, raccoons, or foxes were in the area. There didn't seem to be any other animals close by. This gave them mixed feelings. On one hand they were relieved there were no wild animal close by to surprise them. On the other hand they were upset for the same reason. They wished to communicate with another fox or raccoon.

Buddy lifted his bowed head and pronounced his next intentions. "I think I'll search this mountain for a new home. At least I will be on earth and close to my mother." Bowing his head once more, he whispered, "If I can find such a place." The others agreed to accompany him while they searched for new homes of their own. Being in Colorado, not England, Sly would never find her home. The wise fox knew it was time to adapt.

They searched one path, returned to where there was a fork, and took the other path. One path led to another, and another, and another. They searched and searched, but the mountain looked almost the same no matter what path they traveled. Unless there was a newly shaped boulder, or a stream crossing their path, one course was pretty much identical to the others.

At one stream, the water was extremely wide. It wasn't very deep, but the current was running swiftly over submerged rocks. It reminded Buddy of the larger rapids in Mangonel. Among the rocks, fish were jumping out of the water trying to swim upstream. Buddy remembered his book, and how it showed bears fishing in a stream much like this one. A bear would wade out into the water, and wait for a fish to come along. When the fish jumped out, the bear would catch it in its mouth. Bears are very good at fishing and don't miss very often. Buddy had done some fishing at Balloon Billy's. That time he had been rather successful.

He explained to the others how he was going to catch some fish and asked them to wait on shore. Reviewing his accomplishments in Mangonel, he was confident he would be successful here. The water was cold and as clear and clean as could be. He could see to the bottom with ease. Standing close to one rock, he waited. Then, along came a fish. No, it was many fish. They all started jumping out of the water at the same time. Buddy had no idea which fish to catch. He snatched at one, then another. He tried, and tried, but couldn't catch a single one. This was a great deal harder here on earth than it was in Mangonel, and it was certainly much harder than his book made it look.

While concentrating on his fishing, Buddy failed to notice that another bear arrived at the stream. The new arrival looked angrily at Buddy as he stepped into the water. He found a place he liked, and in seconds had a fish in his mouth. Buddy watched intently to see if he could get any tips from the newcomer. All it took was a bit of timing. He just needed a little practice.

Buddy wanted to ask the other bear if he could teach him how to fish, so he stood straight up, turned to the stranger, and called out to him, "Say there, friend, could you show me how to do this fishing thing? I don't seem to have the hang of it." The other bear stood on his hind legs, raised his front paws high in the air, and growled loudly. He then went onto all fours again and took a short charge toward Buddy.

What is that all about? Buddy thought. *This guy is not at all friendly.* He went back to practicing how to fish on his own. This time he was able to gather a few fish, but he wasn't finished practicing, so he kept fishing a while longer. When he looked up again, there were several more bears in the stream, all of them fishing, all of them catching fish. One bear was very close, so Buddy said hello. This bear looked at Buddy, turned to face him, and let out a low, menacing growl. He wasn't happy to see Buddy either. All these bears were in a bad mood, and none of them spoke to one another.

With all the negative attitudes, Buddy decided to give up fishing for now. He picked up the three large fish he had caught and started toward the bank. The other bears watched him leave. One quickly took over his fishing spot in the creek. When he reached the shore, his friends were nowhere to be found. He called their names, "Sly, Pesky," but there was no answer. He called again. This time when he called, he heard a muffled cry come from the bushes. When he pushed the branches away, he found Sly and Pesky under the paws of yet another bear. "Hurry!" cried Sly. "He is about to eat us."

Buddy couldn't believe what he was hearing, but he knew his friends were in trouble. "Hey, you," he shouted. "Let them go." The bear turned and snarled a warning at Buddy but didn't let Sly or Pesky get up. Buddy was getting very angry now. He was certain his friends were hurting. He was equally certain this bear intended to eat them. Buddy rose up to his full height and growled loudly, "Leave them alone!" This seemed to get the bear's attention. He too stood on his hind legs. He appeared to be measuring up Buddy for a fight. Buddy had grown to his full size by now. He was a head taller than the other bear. His intimidating size drove off the bully. If Buddy hadn't found them, they would have become dinner for that bear. He had saved his companions from certain death.

"What is going on here?" asked Buddy. "Nobody is friendly. Nobody will speak to me. Everyone seems to want to pick a fight. I'm beginning to not like it here."

As was typical, Sly thought she had the answer. "Buddy," she began, "the other animals on earth don't speak in the manner to which we have become accustomed. Each type of animal has its own language. Bears don't speak with raccoons and foxes. Foxes don't speak with bears and raccoons. They have a way of communicating that is limited. Mostly, they spend their time hunting, and competing for food or shelter. When you yelled at that bear, I am sure all he heard was a loud growl. Only Pesky and I know what you said."

"What are you saying? How can that be? I have been a bear a long time now, and I have always been able to speak.

Sly continued, "You can only speak because you are a bear from Mangonel. Bears on earth speak differently and a lot less. Much can be said without words. Think on it Buddy, do you remember ever having a conversation with a bear?"

"No, but I wasn't a bear then."

"Fine, I agree. But why do you suppose these bears on earth paid no attention to your words?"

"I suppose," said Buddy sheepishly, as he knew Sly was right, and now had to admit it, "I suppose they didn't understand me, and only heard a growl like the ones they were making. The only reason they reacted at all is because I am bigger than they are."

Sly smiled. "How true, ol' chap," she said through her grin. "I daresay we will all find our new homes considerably different than what we expected. You can always go back to where your home was, but you must remember, home is where you make it. It is in your heart, Buddy. Home is where you want it to be, where you are comfortable, relaxed, and with family or friends."

"I think I ungrrrstand now," replied Buddy.

"Oh, no," interjected Pesky. "Did you hear that? I think if we stay here much longer, we will also lose our ability to communicate with one another. If we go back to being like all the other animals on earth, Buddy may want to eat us, just like that other bear. I think we should head back to the gate before it's too late."

"I believe you are right about that, Mr. Raccoon," commented Sly. "We really should be off. After this demonstration, I fear we don't have much time before it's too late. Grab the fish, Mr. Bear, before the little thief eats it, *aoooolll*," she howled. She too was changing; her speech was starting to turn to howls.

They ran down the mountainside as fast as safety would allow. This place, earth, was no longer the home they remembered. It was still their childhood home, but it was no longer the home where they wanted to live. It was time to go, and there was no time to dally.

Before they found the swinging stone again, they were all reduced to just a few words they could understand. Buddy didn't speak fox, Sly didn't speak raccoon, and Pesky didn't speak at all. Soon they were not going to be able to understand one another.

Sly called them together in a small circle. "All right, *ahooo*. Sorry about that. We are abaooo to lose touch with IEEEEach other. Here is the plan. We keep oooouurr course to the stone *grrrrrrr* gate. No matter what, keep pushing to the stone. Do you understand me?"

Buddy and Pesky nodded.

They turned in unison and ran for the swinging stone gate. When they reached the spot where they thought the stone should be, it wasn't there. They had taken a wrong turn. Buddy grabbed the two smaller animals under his arms and ran back up the path. It was happening; they couldn't talk to one another. Buddy found one of their guide marks. Then he searched for another farther down the mountain. When he found it, he wasted no time in running headlong down the slope.

There—there it was. Just a bit farther and they would be safe. At that moment, another very large bear stepped into their path. He purposefully blocked their way. Buddy put his friends down and prepared to fight. The big bear was the same size as Buddy. He looked to be just as strong. The newcomer charged straight at Buddy. He slammed his head into Buddy's chest with all his might. They grappled all over the ground. One moment one bear was on top, and then the other obtained the advantage. Dust rose up so thick Sly and Pesky couldn't see them anymore. Growling and snarling, the two combatants tussled on the ground. Suddenly the aggressive bear let go of Buddy. He howled a great howl. Holding his front paws on his backside, he ran off into the forest.

Buddy rose from the ground in surprise. Sly and Pesky stood in the settling dust with large grins on their faces. Pesky was holding a long sharp stick in his paws, and was shoving it back and forth in a stabbing motion. Buddy understood now. Pesky had picked up that stick from someplace and came to his rescue. These two truly were his best friends.

Buddy hugged his companions as hard as he dared. Keeping them in his arms, he went to the stone gate and pushed it so they could pass through. The gate swung easily, just as before.

Once again in Mangonel, they all sat in the grass to gather their senses and strength. After a long, restful pause, Pesky was first to speak. "That was close. Can you guys speak now? Come on, say something."

Buddy shrugged his shoulders before he said, "Sure we can speak. We are in Mangonel, where all sorts of strange things happen."

Just then everything grew dark. A great shadow was passing overhead. Buddy looked up into the sky. They were standing under a huge object floating low in the sky. It was another balloon, like Balloon Billy's, only much larger. It was blue and yellow with a shade of green where the two colors came together. Under the massive balloon was a huge platform. Resting on the platform was a house surrounded by a porch on all sides. The house had large glass doors in the center of each of the four walls. There, on the porch, stood a man. "Hey there, need a lift?" he called.

"Why you old rascal," shouted Buddy. "Where in Mangonel did you get the new balloon?"

"It's a long story," said Billy. "I can tell you along the way. Climb aboard. I have loads of room with this new rig, so you can bring your friends with you."

As they scampered onto the porch, all three were thinking how lucky they were to have such good friends, and to be back in Mangonel, the place they were recently trying to escape. Sure, they were happy to be here, but the thought that stayed with Buddy was, *I wonder if we will ever be able to go back home. In the meantime, I wonder where we're headed to this time.*

Dictionary—Chapter16

Accompany: *To escort or be present with someone else*

Accomplishment: *The successful completion of something*

Accustomed: *Usual, expected because of habits already formed*

Attitude: *An opinion or general feeling*

Combatants: *Fighters*

Communicate: *To talk with someone or give a message in writing*

Dally: *To delay*

Disappointing: *Not meeting what was expected, not as good as you thought*

Extremely: *To a very high degree*

Intentions: *Plans*

Intimidating: *Threatening, frightening*

Navigate: *To find a route or to pass through a place*

Negative: *Unhappy, angry*

Pronounced: *Spoke*

Rascal: *A mischievous person*

Reacted: *Respond to something*

Reduce: *To make smaller*

Sheepishly: *Acting timidly*

Stab: *The thrust of a pointed object*

Submerged: *To be underwater*

Tussled: *Fought*

CHAPTER 17

Billy's New Balloon

Buddy, Sly, and Pesky had narrowly escaped from being trapped on earth. They once longed to be back on earth, but that was when they were unaware of how things had changed for them. Their new home was now the kingdom of Mangonel, but there was no home in Mangonel. These three would have to make their homes wherever they lay their heads. Bound together in friendship and love, they had saved each other's lives. They had become a family of the strangest mixture, a bear, a fox, and a raccoon.

On the day they returned to Mangonel, the oddest thing happened. They met up with Buddy's old acquaintance, Balloon Billy, who offered them a ride. They were now standing on Billy's porch while the entire house floated through the air.

Billy's new balloon was gigantic. It easily carried the house with all is passengers. He was extremely proud of his new design. As he showed his guests the house, he told them that when he left Buddy, so long ago now, he had no control over his balloon. It blew him here and there but never back to his cabin in the mountains. After a while, he decided to make a new house for himself. Since he loved ballooning so much, he figured he might as well make his balloon his house as well. That in turn gave him the idea to build a house on a platform, and to make a new balloon big enough to carry it. This way he was always home, no matter where he went.

The whole idea and engineering of it were ingenious. Surrounding the house was a large porch with a sturdy railing. Billy could float along and view the countryside from any angle. Each of the four walls of the house had a large glass sliding door so he could come in and go out in any direction. He could also open all the doors at once to let in as much fresh air as he liked. In the center of the house was a pot-bellied stove, the chimney of which exited the roof and sent the hot air up into the massive balloon to keep it aloft. In the exposed ceiling joists, Billy secured the old gondola pot. The large pot was now covered it with a heavy lid. Its purpose had changed from gondola to water tank. A pipe ran from the pot to the kitchen sink, which was situated in one corner of the house. To the right of the kitchen were the dining table and one chair. Behind the kitchen chair was a wall of shelves full of food. Next to the shelves, Billy had stacked a pile of wood for the stove, and to the right of that, in the next corner, was a big, overstuffed easy chair. A small end table with a lantern was placed near the easy chair. Some papers with sketches of Billy's design were haphazardly strewn about the table's surface. The last corner of the house was empty, waiting for Billy's next addition, whatever that might be. It was small, but it was comfortably cozy. They all thought Billy's new place was grand.

"Where to?" asked Billy.

"What kind of question is that?" Sly inquired. "You have just now stated that you have no control over this contraption, and that you have no idea where the wind will take us. How can you ever believe you will be able to fulfill a request for one destination or another?"

"One can only try, Miss Fox; one can only try," replied Billy.

Buddy tried to recall the map Ryla had drawn in the cave floor, but his memory failed him. His recollection was sketchy at best. Sly asked what he was thinking, and when he explained, Sly, in a hushed voice, offered her thoughts. "I think I know where we can get a map, if one exists." She went over to the provisions bag, and in a moment she returned with a folded parchment. They all went to the kitchen table and spread the weathered map across it for everyone to see. The paper and drawing looked very old. The edges were frayed and discolored, but the center, with the exceptions of a few tears at the folds, was in excellent shape. The map showed all the towns and landmarks Ryla had drawn in the sand of her cave but with much more detail. Buddy recognized the places he had been and pointed them out to the group. All the towns and places of importance were very clear. It seemed the closer they examined the map, the more detail they found. The remainder of the map had a monotone appearance, like that of an old seafarer's chart, or a pirate's treasure map. Whoever had drawn this chart knew the kingdom of Mangonel exceptionally well.

After closer inspection, Buddy and Billy both pointed to a spot on the map. They were indicating where they were at that moment. With the map to help them, they could follow along as they passed over recognizable objects below. Because of the way the map was drawn, that would be a very easy task.

Sly looked at their new chart of Mangonel, closed her eyes and drew haphazard circles around the map. She stopped circling, stuck out her paw, and randomly pointed to a spot on the map. "There, we should go there," she said, opening her eyes. The place she pointed to was named Picture Palace. "That looks interesting," she stated. "Let's be off."

Billy put a log or two into the stove. With the increase in heat, the balloon began to rise higher. The direction they wanted, once again, was east.

The balloon rose up for a few minutes and began heading in their desired easterly direction. According to the map, it looked as though they were going to fly directly over a lake called Fairy Lake. From there they would head into the low mountain range where the Picture Palace was supposed to be.

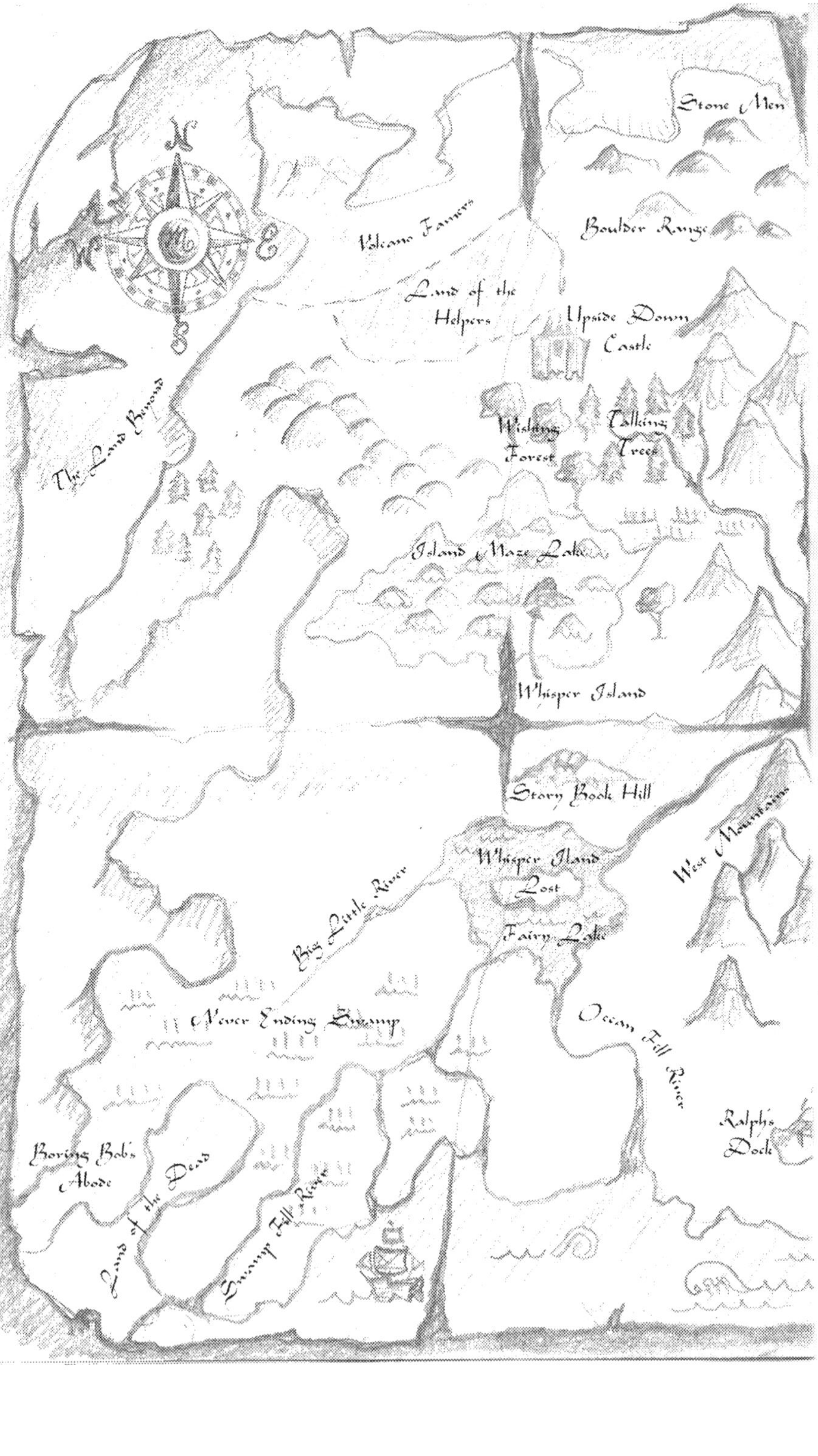
N
E
W
S
Stone Men
Boulder Range
Volcano Farmers
Land of the Helpers
Upside Down Castle
Wishing Forest
Talking Trees
The Land Beyond
Island Maze Lake
Whisper Island
Story Book Hill
West Mountains
Whisper Island Lost
Fairy Lake
Big Little River
Never Ending Swamp
Ocean Fall River
Ralph's Dock
Boring Bob's Abode
Land of the Dead
Swamp Fall River

The Forbidden Lands

Rhyne

Hairy

Hidden River of Life

Spring

Balders

Ho Hum Home

Fable Forest

Frigid Flat

Hide Village

The Pointers

Picky People Plat

Village of No Roofs

The Bubble People

I-M's

Pointing Isles

Dangerous Desert

Balloon Billy

Silent Sea

River River

Giant Falls

Cabin of Pencil Packin Pete

East Mountains

South River River

Serpentine River

No Place Place

Ralph's Path

Falls End

Ralph The Raft Man

Tipsy Town

The Great Salt Ocean

The map didn't have a legend to tell them the distances between landmarks or towns, so they just sort of guessed. In Mangonel, a place may look to be close and yet be very, very far away, or it could be just the opposite. There was no way of knowing. The best thing to do was to accept what is, and move on. After all, they were no longer anxious to find a way home, so there was no rush to go anywhere special. They had to adopt the idea that wherever they went, that place was going to be where they were headed. They were adventurers, explorers, and vagabonds. Their new quest was to see as much of Mangonel as they could, maybe find the ruler of this kingdom, and ask him a whole lot of questions. This new life, without the pressure of finding a way home, lessened their anxiety. The three grew more cheerful, easygoing, and downright happy with every passing moment. Of course they were also dry and in no danger at the moment, which helped their mood immensely.

As the balloon rose higher, the wind shifted. Apparently, Ryla had other plans for them. Instead of heading east, they began heading nearly due north. A glance at the map made Buddy cringe. It looked as though they were heading straight for the Land of the Helpers.

This was not at all where Buddy wanted to go. The others thought it would be great, since they had not been there before. When Buddy explained his experience, the rest of them laughed and laughed. Still, they thought it might be fun to have so much help. They just didn't understand that too much of a good thing can ruin it.

The balloon passed over some plains with golden grasses waving in the breeze. They were high enough to see a few other towns or villages as they sailed across the sky. Far below, there was an enormous lake of crystal clear, green water. Even from their height they could see the fish swimming around, but that was not as strange as the number of islands that dotted the lake. There must have been thousands of them. Buddy imagined he was in a boat in the middle of that lake. Immediately he knew it would be as bad as being in the middle of the Never-Ending Swamp. Getting out would be next to impossible.

Far off to the right, they could see the tops of the mountains. The map identified the mountains as the Major Mountains. This piqued Balloon Billy's interest. "That's where my old cabin is located. Let me see that map."

Sure enough, when he looked carefully at the map, searching the Major Mountains, he found the spot where his cabin used to be. "Now that is a curious thing," he said. "This map looks real old, and yet my cabin is shown on it."

Buddy and Sly stared at the map, trying to locate the places they had visited. All of the places were there, together with many locations they had yet to visit. As Buddy stared at the map he thought of Ryla and her cave. A mark appeared in the mountains with an identifier indicating where the Cave of Wonders was located. By this time, Buddy was forming some ideas in his head. *This must be a magical map. When I look at the chart I can see where others have traveled, and I can see where I have been.*

Buddy poked Sly. "Can you see Ryla's cave? Look, it's right there," he pointed.

"Yes, it wasn't there before," she replied.

"Ahhhh! I think I get it," offered Buddy. "You see, if someone has been to a place, and concentrates on the map, the map adds it all by itself. This is a magical map. All the other places on the map must have been visited by others and added to the scroll as time passed." He looked at Billy. "Both you and I were at your cabin. When we looked at the map, your cabin must have been added."

A look of worry came over Sly's face. "We had better take special care of this map and our provisions bag. Who knows what other magic it may contain?"

Billy's head popped up from the map to stare at Sly, "You have a provisions bag, a super sack? My, oh my!" he said.

Now Sly was really worried. She had revealed the one secret they were trying so hard to conceal. That bag was said to be one of the most valuable treasures in the kingdom, and there was no telling what others might do to get their hands on it. Billy could possibly change from a friend to terrible foe. Since Sly was the one to reveal the secret, she was determined to keep a careful eye on Billy until they parted company.

That night, while everyone was sleeping, Sly secretly watched as Billy crept over to the provisions bag. He hovered over the bag for a long time before he removed something. Sly didn't sleep the entire night after that.

The next morning, when everyone else awoke, Ryla had stopped blowing. The big balloon didn't move one way or another; it simply hovered in one place. They all went over to the porch railings and looked down. Seeing they were close to a castle, they raced to the map. This castle was upside down. Buddy remembered seeing it the last time he and Billy passed this way.

"Put us on the ground, please," Buddy requested.

Touching Buddy's arm to get his attention, Sly said, "Wait one moment." Then she turned to Billy. "I know you took something from our bag last night. Please return it."

Billy was embarrassed. He shuffled from one foot to the next. Finally he reached in his pocket, pulled out a sheet of paper, and handed it to Sly.

Sly turned the paper over. It was a picture of Billy's old cabin with his old balloon parked beside it. "I'm sorry," said Billy. "I know I will never see my old place again. I just wanted a remembrance of it. I knew I couldn't get a picture from anywhere else, so I took it from your bag. Please forgive me; I should have asked. You can have the picture back; it isn't worth our friendship. We can still be friends, can't we?"

Sly was a little embarrassed now. "Sure, we are still friends. Taking the picture is not a problem. Please keep it. Besides, it was partially my fault for letting it be known that we have the bag. However, I must point out, you were correct, you should have asked first. Now, let's put this all behind us. Please put us on the ground, as Buddy requested." Then she thought of something else, pulled Buddy and Pesky into a circle, and stated, "Since we are all friends, and we have a secret to share, we must all take the pinky oath never to tell anyone of the provisions bag again. This includes you, Billy. Come join our circle of friends."

They all agreed. The provisions bag was indeed a precious secret. There was no question that it must remain so. Standing in a circle, they all clasped their pinkies together and followed Sly's cue: "I pinky swear never to tell anyone about the provisions bag that Buddy Bear possesses." They all repeated the oath. Sly added one more statement. "If I ever give up this secret and break the oath, the punishment will be to lose these friends forever. Wherever I go, I will have to tell everyone I meet that I am not a trustworthy friend." That did it. Now they were all certain to keep their promise.

Billy set the house on the ground so lightly they thought they were still floating. As they departed, Billy gave them a wink and said, "I am off to find the treasures of Mangonel." He then went into the house, stoked the potbelly stove, and the balloon rose again into the sky. Soon, Ryla began to blow a steady breeze that carried Billy farther to the north.

The three travelers waved good-bye. Then they turned to stare at the upside-down castle. Having second thoughts about going into this new place, they thought that perhaps it would be better to bypass the castle altogether. After all, there were many other places in the kingdom of Mangonel to explore. There was no doubt there were other strange and interesting places to visit. They didn't have to go into the intimidating castle. They had no business there, and their new map promised that there were many other, less scary, adventures. However, they were here, at the castle. Maybe they would finally meet the king of this kingdom.

Buddy told the others, "We are going to the castle. The king should be able to help us in any number of ways."

Dictionary—Chapter 17

Acquaintance: *Someone who is known only slightly*

Anxiety: *Feeling worried*

Aplenty: *More than enough*

Clasp: *To hold tightly with hands or arms*

Conceal: *To hide from view*

Concentrate: *Devote a significant effort or thoughts on one subject*

Contraption: *A device or machine that looks strange*

Countryside: *Open property outside the limits of a city*

Cringe: *Crouch or move back suddenly*

Determined: *Strong minded*

Discolored: *Changed from the original color*

Embarrassed: *Self-conscious*

Engineering: *To apply the science of designing things*

Enormous: *Very large*

Extremely: *A very high degree*

Foe: *Enemy*

Frayed: *Wearing away of the edge or surface of cloth, rope, paper, etc., from friction*

Gigantic: *Overly large*

Gondola: *A cart or basket attached to a hot air balloon*

Haphazard: *Unplanned*

Hover: *To float in the air and without moving in any direction*

Identifier: *A symbol that gives clues to what something is*

Immense: *Very large*

Importance: *Having significant meaning*

Indicate: *To point something out*

Ingenious: *Clever*

Landmark: *Something that marks and identifies a specific location*

Legend: *A chart showing a scale to measure distances*

Longed: *Desired, wanted*

Mixture: *A combining of different things*

Monotone: *Without much variation in color or tone*

Narrowly: *A very small margin*

Overstuffed: *To fill beyond normal capacity*

Parchment: *A yellowish colored material made from dried animal skins and used for paper*

Partially: *Some, incomplete*

Pinky: *The little finger*

Pique: *Arouse*

Potbelly stove: *A round stove wherein the fuel is burned within a round container, creating a platform for cooking*

Randomly: *Without a pattern*

Recollection: *To remember something*

Remembrance: *An item to be remembered*

Revealed: *To make something visible that had been hidden or covered*

Seafarer: *Someone who goes to sea in ships*

Scroll: *A roll of parchment or paper used for a written document*

Shuffled: *To walk without lifting the feet*

Sketchy: *Lacking in substance or clarity*

Stoked: *To excite or exhilarate the flames of a fire*

Unaware: *Unknown*

Vagabond: *A homeless wanderer*

CHAPTER 18

Upside-Down Castle

The three friends found themselves standing in a field outside the walls of the upside down castle. The strangeness of it didn't strike Buddy as severely as it did the others. (Of course this was not Buddy's first glimpse of this crazy structure.) It didn't make much difference; they were all wondering what kind of place this was. The entire castle was built upside-down. Most castles are built on higher ground; this castle was built at the bottom of a hill. Everything seemed to be opposite of what is normally expected.

The group walked up to the stone walls that surrounded the castle, and then they walked all the way around it to see if they could find some sort of entrance. They found none. Buddy looked at his raccoon friend and asked, "Pesky, you are pretty good at getting into places. Do you think you could use your skills to get us inside?"

Pesky puffed up his chest. "Sure, if there is a way in, I'll find it," and he scampered off toward the castle walls.

A few minutes later, the raccoon returned with a big grin on his face. "Found it; follow me," was all he said.

Pesky led them to a place along the walls where there was no opening, no door, or gate. "Where?" asked Sly. "I see no passage for entry."

Pesky's smile broadened. He walked over to the wall and placed his paw against one of the larger stones. His whole arm went right through it. That one stone was an illusion. It looked solid enough, but when you got really close, you could see through it like a fine curtain. Proudly, Pesky offered, "This way if you please," and bowed for the others to pass.

Even though the outside of the castle was upside-down, the inside was right side up. However, upon entering the castle, they were whisked away from the floor to the ceiling. On their way up, they were turned upside-down so their feet landed on the ceiling. It was a strange sensation. The small bench and table that sat in this entryway were somehow stuck to the floor, so they didn't rise up. Walking around the room, there was nothing in their way. The ceiling was empty, but they were using it like it was a floor. Buddy remembered being in his bed, looking at the ceiling and imagining what it would be like to walk around up there instead of on the floor. Here, in this castle, he was doing that very thing.

It wasn't long before a guard came barging into the entry chamber. He was huge. His head was encased in a shiny helmet that covered most of his face. His large chest was protected by a metal armored breastplate that hung over his shoulders. His arms were massive mounds of muscle. In one hand he carried a shield, and in the other he held a short sword. He wore a thick leather skirt that was secured to his knees with leather straps. He wore sandals that covered his calves like shin guards.

There was no joy in his manner as he approached. Loudly, he inquired, "What are you doing here? How dare you enter this castle without invitation?" He stared at them for a moment and then said, "I should run you all through with this sword, but King Garindrake the Kind will want to speak with you first. Go ahead of me so I can keep an eye on you. I will tell you which way to go."

The companions turned down one corridor and up another as they followed the guard's instructions. They climbed some stairs and went down others. The path the guard took them on was full of twists and turns, as well as a myriad of ups and downs. All the turns, combined with having to travel upside down along the ceiling, confused them to the point where they would have been hopelessly lost without the guard.

By the time they were ushered into the great hall to see King Garindrake, they all had headaches from their blood going to their heads. The king entered the large room and turned a knob on the wall. As he rotated the knob, everyone slowly turned right side up. They drifted to the floor where benches were set, and the king's royal seat sat on a raised platform. King Garindrake walked to his chair and sat. Looking at the three standing before him, he motioned them to approach.

When they got to the base of the platform, they stopped. It was easy to see the king from here. He was a large man, like the guard, maybe even larger.

"Please get chairs for our guests," he softly requested the guard. In a booming voice, he finally addressed his visitors, "You are the newcomers to Mangonel I have heard about, are you not?"

"Yes, I suppose so," said Buddy.

"Ah, I have been hoping you would come this way. I love adventures and a good story. You will tell me of your travels, and when finished, you will stay as my guests."

Pesky couldn't hold back his awe and spoke. "Are you the king of Mangonel?"

"Ha, ha, ha, ha, ha, ha!" The king laughed. "The king of Mangonel; that is a good one. No, I am only the appointed king of this castle. There has been no king of Mangonel for centuries." Seeing the look of disappointment on their faces, he continued, "Let me explain. A long, long time ago, a powerful man of magic named Zandordrake was cast into this place now known as Mangonel. He was a wizard. A very powerful wizard. Zandordrake, a distant cousin to the Great Merlin, was also one of Merlin's apprentices. Zandordrake possessed the greatest amount of magic of all the apprentices, and Merlin hoped that Zandordrake would someday take his place. However, during a fit of rage, Zandordrake misused his magical powers. He cast an unthinkable spell upon the people.

Merlin couldn't break the spell because Zandordrake cast it in haste. Mispronouncing and slurring the words together altered the spell so that it couldn't be broken. Merlin, no longer able to trust his cousin, banished him from the land, and sent him here through a porthole known only to Merlin. Zandordrake's banishment was magically sealed by the great magician so he could never return to earth.

"In the beginning Zandordrake hated this place. There was no one here, just Zandordrake. As time passed, in order to have some companionship, he used his magic to allow the animals to speak. He made it so some trees could speak and cast a spell for some trees to walk. In order to preserve his magic, he cast a spell on an entire forest. In the event he could no longer remember something, all he had to do was wish the trees to remind him. This was perfectly well and good, but he wanted human companionship. He searched the land up and down but found no one. The searching made for a lot of walking. Zandordrake began to create magical portholes of his own that would carry him from one place in Mangonel to another. Those gates gave him the idea to construct gates that connected to earth. Even though he couldn't get back to Earth, he could open gates from earth to here. It was his hope that someone might stumble into this land through his magical openings. As it turned out, many people did.

"During his time in Mangonel, Zandordrake found he needed many things he could not get here, so he made what he called his Merlin's bag. The bag held everything. A bit absentminded, he misplaced several of these before he died. It is said they still exist somewhere in the kingdom.

"Zandordrake was the most powerful man in the land, and without any opposition, he proclaimed himself king. As king, he claimed all the land as his own. He proclaimed this new land to be his kingdom of Mangonel. The name comes from a type of catapult that was used during his time on earth. Since he was sort of catapulted here by Merlin, he felt the name appropriate.

"Zandordrake, after years of searching, finally gave up. He decided he needed a permanent home, and his kingdom needed a castle. He created this castle with magic, but once again, his impatience caused a mix up in the spell, and the castle was formed upside down. All the furniture was permanently affixed by the same bad spell.

"As you can imagine, living here was difficult for Zandordrake. By the time he figured out how to reverse the gravity, he was too weak to correct the entire castle. Only some places have the knobs that permit normal use of the room.

"During the long years after Zandordrake's passing, the castle was occupied by many different people. Most did not adapt to the upside-down way of life. I, on the other hand, as a distant relative of Zandordrake, though I have no magical powers, have adapted very well. Those who stay here look to me as the king of this castle. Their service to me is rewarded with the safety and food this fortress provides. It took a considerable amount of time, but eventually, those who remain within the castle became accustomed to being upside-down for long periods.

"That, my friends, is the long and short of it." The king's stomach growled. "It is growing late, and I am hungry." He called the guard, and rather than command, like you would believe a king would, he asked, "Quinbeck, would you be so kind as to show our guests to their room? Allow them to freshen up, and then escort them to the dining hall." He turned to his guests again, "You can tell me of your adventures over dinner." Then he departed without another word.

Quinbeck, the guard, motioned for them to follow. Again, they were led through twisted halls, and up and down stairs. The entire journey to their room was spent dangling from the ceiling. If it were not for the headaches that came so rapidly, it might have been an exciting experience. When they reached their guest quarters, the room was still upside down, and there was no switch to turn off the anti-gravity. In the bathroom, they had to push off the ceiling to the sink, turn on the water, and catch it before it rose up to the ceiling.

After washing up, they followed Quinbeck to the dining hall. The hall had a switch, so when they entered they were all turned right-side up. The food upon the table was in great abundance, but there was something oddly familiar. Buddy was sure he had seen the table, the chairs, and even the utensils. As they began to eat, one of the people at the table suggested they eat their food very fast, because not too long ago, just as the table was set, it all disappeared. A few hours later it came back with four dirty place settings, and some of the food had been eaten.

Buddy and Sly now knew where they had seen this table; it was at Pencil-Packin' Pete's. This was the table that appeared in his front yard after he had written his request on a pad. That would mean the tree, and the dinner at Pete's, and everything else he has delivered to his house, is taken from someone or somewhere else in Mangonel. Sly whispered to Buddy, "Yet another example that nothing is free. I wonder if our provisions bag operates in the same manner."

They ate heartily, all the while telling the king and his guests about all they had seen and done in Mangonel. Everyone was delighted with their stories. They couldn't get enough. After each tale the people at the table begged for more until Buddy, Sly, and even Pesky were so tired they could hardly speak.

King Garindrake the Kind clapped his hands, which signaled the waiters to start cleaning up the table. Buddy apologized for having to ask to be excused for the evening. He asked if Quinbeck could show them to their room. The king understood and dismissed the entire gathering.

Back in their bed chamber, they discovered it was remarkably comfortable for sleeping. All they had to do was lie horizontally. The antigravity made them as light as a feather. Slowly they floated to the ceiling. There was no bed, but there was no need for one. It was like sleeping on a bed of air. In fact, that was exactly what they were doing. There was no pressure on any part of their bodies because there was no mattress, no bed, no cushion, and no pillow. Reclining in the air, the blood didn't go to their heads. This was the most comfortable night any of them had ever had. If it were not for the headaches, they might have stayed to serve this king like the others who dwelt there.

In the morning they awoke as rested as could be. They were refreshed; ready for almost anything. When they opened the door, they found Quinbeck standing guard. *Has he been there all night?* Pesky wondered. *Was he guarding to keep us in, or to keep others out?* But he said, "Good morning, Quinbeck! How was your night?"

"Fine, follow me please," said the unpleasant guard without any emotion whatsoever.

They were expecting to be led to the dining hall again for breakfast, but instead he led them to the exit door. This was certainly a surprise.

Sly looked up at the big man. "Did we do something to offend King Garindrake?" she asked. "Why are we being escorted out?"

"No, my lady, you did nothing wrong. The king was most pleased to have had you as his guests;, everyone was. However, there is a rule here that forbids anyone from staying more than one night, unless they swear lifelong allegiance to the king. Too often visitors have come here, refused to leave, and became permanent guests. They offered no help and were a burden to everyone else. Because they would not leave on their own, King Garindrake had to ask them to leave. When this happens, guests depart angrily. People who might have become good friends were lost because of their greed and misunderstanding of the king. Therefore, King Garindrake the Kind set rules in place to avoid this unpleasantness. Now please, depart in good standing and as welcomed friends. Oh, yes, his majesty also wishes me to convey to you that you are welcome to return should you pass this way again."

Quinbeck nearly shoved them through the opening. Once on the outside of the castle walls, the large stone that hid the entrance became more solid. Pesky touched the stone just as they heard the clanging of what sounded like a lock. "It's as solid as the rest of the wall," he remarked in a tone of finality.

"Strange," said Buddy.

Sly looked at Buddy with a faraway look and said, "Not as strange as some other things we have come across in Mangonel, and probably not as strange as some things we are bound to encounter in the future."

"How true, how true," replied Buddy. "However, it now appears it is time for us to be on our way."

Dictionary—Chapter 18

Absentminded: *Forgetful*

Abundance: *A large amount*

Adapt: *Change to meet the conditions that exist at that time*

Affix: *Attach*

Allegiance: *Loyalty to someone, giving devoted support*

Alter: *To make changes to something*

Appointed: *Chosen*

Apprentice: *Someone studying a trade under an expert*

Appropriate: *Fitting, suitable for the occasion*

Armored: *Equipped with a protective metal covering*

Awe: *A feeling of amazement and respect*

Banished: *To be cast out into exile, not allowed to ever return*

Barging: *Moving roughly*

Breastplate: *A piece of armor that covers the chest*

Broadened: *Made wider*

Catapult: *A medieval machine used to launch large stones to break down castle walls*

Chamber: *A room used for a particular purpose*

Convey: *To pass along an idea*

Corridor: *A passageway or hallway*

Dangling: *Hanging loosely*

Disappointment: *A feeling of being let down*

Dwelt: *Resided, lived in an area*

Encased: *To surround something completely*

Escorted: *To be accompanied by another*

Finality: *The quality of being the end or final action*

Forbid: *Order someone not to do something*

Gravity: *The attraction due to the earth's rotation*

Haste: *Great speed; to act quickly*

Heartily: *In a sincere and enthusiastic way*

Horizontally: *Level, parallel to the ground seen in the distance*

Illusion: *A false idea or conception of something, something that looks like one thing but is really something else.*

Imagine: *To form a picture in the mind*

Impatience: *Annoyance. Not wishing to wait*

Manner: *The way something is done or how it happens*

Massive: *Extremely large, solid, and heavy*

Misplaced: *To lose something, especially through forgetfulness*

Mispronouncing: *Saying your words incorrectly*

Misunderstanding: *A lack of comprehension*

Misuse: *The incorrect or improper use of something*

Motioned: *A signal to somebody as a request or to bring attention to something*

Myriad: *A very large number of something*

Occupy: *Live or stay in one place*

Opening: *A gap or hole in something*

Opposition: *A negative attitude or action to keep something from happening*

Passage: *A pathway through an obstruction*

Porthole: *A small opening in a fortified wall*

Proclaim: *To declare something for everyone to hear*

Permanent: *Lasting forever, never changing*

Scamper: *To run quickly or playfully*

Sensation: *A physical feeling or mental perception*

Severely: *To a greater degree*

Slurring: *Speaking indistinctly so that your words cannot be understood*

Strangeness: *The condition of being oddly different*

Stumble: *To trip over something*

Unthinkable: *Beyond the imagination*

Usher: *To be taken someplace by another person*

Wizard: *A myth of someone who is supposed to have magical or wonder-working powers*

CHAPTER 19

Volcano Farmers

Upon leaving the upside-down castle, there seemed to be little else that would surprise Buddy, Sly, or Pesky in this kingdom of Mangonel. Their short stay within the castle gave them a great deal of information about this unusual land. They now understood it was more magical than it was odd. There was a history to much they had already discovered. What they had learned would probably explain many things they would encounter in the future.

It was decided that since they were no longer on a quest to find a way home, there was no rush to continue their search for a gate in the easterly portion of the kingdom. With that settled, the group of friends examined their map and headed north. Buddy was quick to remind them about his experience in the Land of the Helpers. He also expressed his desire to never pass that way again.

Traveling north led them past the yellow gate that Buddy had stumbled upon many months earlier. Mr. Patrick Michael

McDougal Oshay was pleased to see Buddy, but he was so engrossed in his work he didn't stop to chat. He kept on painting and snatching at the recently painted handle. No matter how quickly he jerked the gate open in his never-ending attempt to catch the culprit who kept messing up his fresh paint, the prankster was always able to elude capture. As the threesome passed by, Mr. Patrick Michael McDougal Oshay commented to Buddy, "Ya see, laddie? Just ye luke on thet. The sneaky lil' leprechaun jis wheel no stoop with his wee joke."

Buddy replied with a big grin on his face, "Keep at it, Mr. Oshay, you'll catch him eventually."

It wasn't long before Buddy could see the silhouette of the Land of the Helpers on the horizon. The thought of entering that place gave him the shivers. "Let's give this town a wide berth," he cautioned his friends as he turned to his right. They kept the town in sight but never got any closer for fear someone might see them and come running out to help them along their way.

Once they were on the opposite side of the Land of the Helpers, they turned right once more to continue on their way northward. The map they had taken from their Merlin's bag wasn't much help because it showed nothing in the area beyond the Helpers village. Who knew what lay ahead? Some places were indicated on the map; others were not. It all depended on who had held the map and where they had traveled. If nobody had ever come this far north, nothing would be shown on the map. Then again, there may not be anything in this northern part of Mangonel. There was little to do except carry on in the spirit of the adventure.

A short while after they passed the Land of the Helpers, the ground started to rise in elevation. It rose slowly at first, then more steeply as they traveled, making their walk more labored than when they were on the level plains. Upon reaching the top, they scanned their surroundings. They were standing on the top of a huge ring of raised ground. This ring surrounded a great depression, like a circular valley in a group of mountains. The ring was so large it was difficult to see the other side. In the center was yet another ring of raised ground. The inner circle wasn't anywhere near as high as the outer ring where the travelers were standing. Since they were on the highest ground, they were able to see inside the inner circle, and to their surprise, there lay a tiny community.

Pesky jumped with joy. "Now we are on an adventure!" he exclaimed. "Let's go see if they have anything to eat."

Sly wasn't so happy for some reason. She stated her uneasiness to Buddy with a word of caution. "There is something I don't like about this place," she said. "I'm not sure what it is just yet, but my senses tell me it may be best to turn around. My instincts are warning of a danger here, or maybe we are not welcome."

"We will be extra cautious then," was Buddy's confident reply.

Pesky entered the discussion. "Perhaps your wariness is due to this location. I've seen a place like this before. It's the remains of an old volcano. This one must have been enormous. I too sense a danger, but I believe it's from the minor shaking of the ground. This volcano isn't entirely dead."

Now all three travelers were worried about being in this area of Mangonel. There was no wondering why there was no spot marked on the map showing this place. Who would come here? It was risky business to be anywhere near this place for very long, even if the people living in the middle circle proved to be hospitable.

"Do you suppose the occupants of that little farming community in the center of this volcano are aware of the danger?" questioned Sly. "If they are not, I would think it terribly negligent of us not to warn them, don't you?"

The others succumbed to Sly's assessment of the situation. Without another word or moment's delay, they began descending the rim of the outer circle. The inner, smaller circle was an easy climb. When they reached the rim they could see all the people going about their business of farming. Shovels, rakes, hoes, pitchforks, and sickles were flinging dirt and plants in all directions. Some people were on their hands and knees pulling weeds, some were picking the vegetables from the plants and placing them in baskets, and some were gathering the baskets full of the freshly picked crops. It looked like a chaotic mess, but in reality they were all working together like a well-oiled machine.

They were so engrossed in watching the farming activity they didn't notice a young child approach them. When he spoke, all three jumped with a start.

"Jello," said the boy in a sing-song way. "Whaaaat are hue doing hee-ah? Wee nevah haffa vishators."

Buddy took a step forward and spoke to the boy. The child was about six or seven years old, small in height, and frail looking. His most striking features were his almond-shaped eyes and a long braided ponytail that hung from the back of his shaved head. "Hello," said Buddy, "We are travelers, adventurers of the kingdom of Mangonel. If we approach your community, will we be welcome?"

"Hy," said the boy. "I tin so."

"Hello again," said Buddy. "Could you lead us? That way the people will know we are friendly."

Once again the boy said, "Hy," as he made a little bow of his head.

"Hi," said Buddy, and he looked at Sly with a funny grin. He asked with his eyes, *What is with all the hellos?*

On the way down the slope, Buddy continued to speak with the boy. "What is your name?"

Proudly the boy announced he was called, "Chow Fling."

As Buddy pointed to himself and the others, he said, "We are Buddy, Sly, and Pesky, pleased to meet you. Do you and your people know you are living in a volcano?"

"Hy," said the boy.

"Yes, yes, hello. Do you know it's dangerous to live here? You really should move your village out of this area in case the volcano blows up again. It's already shaking the ground."

This time the young fellow replied, "No. Nobody wanna go."

"The volcano could erupt at any minute," argued Buddy.

"Hy."

Finally, Buddy understood the boy would answer no to some questions and hy to others. He surmised that hy was their word for yes. It was equally clear that the boy understood what Buddy was saying.

"You seem to understand me," Buddy commented. "So, can you tell me why you wish to stay here?'

"Hy. Me talky hue langish good. We stay hee cause dirt he-a is good. Grow big many food. Besta evva." By the looks of the crops, the boy was telling the truth. These people knew how to farm and were experts in choosing the choicest soil for the greatest yield. They knew what they were doing, and they did it very well.

It took a long time to go the short distance down to where the farmers were. They were following a boy who took very small steps. His wooden-sandaled feet were small, and as he walked, the tightly gathered robes he wore caused him to take baby steps.

Getting closer to the farmers, Buddy noticed the entire group of people wore the same type of robes and wooden sandals. Their wardrobe was a copy of what they were accustomed to while on earth. Their short steps, caused by their restrictive clothing, didn't seem to bother them. Buddy understood the significance of their traditions and respected the farmers for holding on to them. Knowing one's past helps one to know who one is. These people understood the importance of their heritage.

Everyone in the town was involved with their work. They didn't see the boy or his invitees until they were nearly in the garden area. One woman saw their shadow as they approached. She glanced up and shrieked in freight. It didn't take long for the remaining men and women to rise from their tasks to see what was happening. One man grabbed his pitchfork from the ground and began shouting, "Hue go! We no likey anyboody he-a. Hue go way!" The man paused for a reaction from the travelers. Seeing none, he continued, "We no wan you hee. Hue go now." When Buddy and his band didn't turn to leave immediately, the man hollered something to the others in his own language. "Chee-ahhg. Aaaaaa i i eeeeeee!" he yelled, which in English means, "Charge! Aaaaaa i i eeeeeee!" They all began to advance toward Buddy, Sly, and Pesky in an effort to chase them away.

"I think we are not as welcome as you thought," Sly commented to the boy.

Chow Fling just stared at them. Shyly, he replied, "Hy."

At this point, there was no alternative but to run away. In just a few steps, they could hear the clamor of the crowd receding. Buddy thought they had given up the chase. He turned around to see what was happening, and what he saw made him laugh. The entire community had turned out for the chase, but with their clothing wrapped so tightly around their ankles, they were forced to take tiny steps. No matter how fast they tried to run, they never went very fast or very far. For every step Buddy took, the farmers had to take fifteen or more. There was no rush to leave. A brisk walk out of the valley kept them well clear of any trouble.

The next time they looked back, they saw the boy was following them. He had ripped his clothing all the way up to his knees and was now running toward them. Sly, Buddy, and Pesky stopped to wait for him. When the youngster caught up, he apologized for the town's behavior.

"So solly! Solly we upset evvaone. Alla dem, dey afeared wiff strangas. Dey haff bad time. Hue unnastan?"

"Hy," said Buddy.

"Good. People haffa come in past. Dey break alla stuff. Dey kill alla plants. Dey bigga bad. Old ones rememba. Dey no likey any mo peoples any mo. Solly! You go now," explained Chow Fling.

"That's all right. We understand, and thank you for explaining," offered Sly. "Please, when you return, warn the good people of your village there is danger living in this valley. Warn them about the volcano. Try to get them to leave here before it's too late."

Chow gave his usual answer, "Hy." He started to leave but turned after a few steps. "I likey new clothes. I go fass now. Hue big nice for me. Thank hue," he said with a grin.

Sly called back, "You're welcome, but don't forget your traditions."

The adventurers did an about face to continue their exit march. When they reached the taller ridgeline, they looked back for the last time. The farmers were not chasing them anymore, but they had not returned to their gardening. Obviously they wanted the intruders to depart completely.

Buddy congratulated Sly and Pesky on their premonitions. Their concerns regarding the possibility of trouble had been proved to be accurate. Then the big bear commented on the fact that even though the people were not all that friendly, and it seemed they had good reason not to be, he was still worried about the villagers' safety.

Yet again, Buddy and his pals were faced with what had become a permanent question here in Mangonel: *"Where to now?"*

Pesky suggested, "I say we continue heading east. Is that all right with you?"

Buddy and Sly made a little bow toward the raccoon. Together they replied, "Hy."

Dictionary—Chapter 19

Admired: *Pleased by somebody*

Alternative: *A different way of doing something*

Assessment: *A judgment based on the known facts*

Attempt: *Try to do something*

Chaotic: *Complete disorder, out of control*

Clamor: *A great amount of noise*

Congratulate: *Express pleasure at somebody's good fortune*

Culprit: *The accused person, the person who caused a problem*

Depend: *To rely on something or someone*

Depression: *A hollowed-out area*

Descending: *Going down*

Desire: *To wish for something*

Elevation: *The height above a location, generally height above sea level*

Eluded: *To escape or avoid*

Engross: *To occupy your attention*

Erupt: *Explode or burst suddenly*

Expert: *Someone skilled or who has great knowledge in something*

Hospitable: *Friendly, treating visitors well*

Immediately: *At once*

Indicated: *To point to something, to show the truth in something*

Instinct: *Strong natural impulse, an inborn pattern of behavior*

Invitees: *People who were asked to attend or join in*

Labored: *Worked hard*

Negligent: *Careless more often than not, irresponsible*

Occupants: *People who live in a place*

Obviously: *Clearly, undoubtedly*

Premonition: *Having a feeling regarding the future*

Quest: *A search for something, an adventurous expedition*

Receding: *To fall back*

Restrictive: *Acting to limit something*

Scan: *To look at something quickly*

Senses: *Physical faculties like hearing, taste, touch*

Shiver: *To tremble with fear or cold*

Sickle: *A tool for cutting grass or wheat*

Shriek: *To make a shrill sound*

Significance: *Importance*

Silhouette: *The shadowed contour of something*

Situation: *The state of affairs, current circumstances*

Stumble: *To trip over*

Succumb: *To give in*

Summarize: *A shortened version of something said, written, or done*

Tradition: *Customs or beliefs handed down from generation to generation*

Uneasiness: *Uncomfortable feeling*

Wariness: *Cautious and alert*

Wardrobe: *All the clothes belonging to one person*

Wide berth: *To give something plenty of room*

Yield: *Produce, the results from an effort*

CHAPTER 20

Stone Men

The Volcano Farmers, living in the belly of a nearly dormant volcano, had chased Buddy and his companions from their caldera. Buddy and Sly warned Chow Fling of the dangers his village could encounter while living in the belly of a volcano, and they hoped Chow would be able to convince the farmers to leave before another eruption occurred.

At the bottom of the tall hillside that surrounded the inside of the volcano, and the farmers' community, the three friends decided they had little interest in going south again. They had just come from that direction, so they turned to the east, thus beginning the next leg on their quest for adventure.

Heading east would allow them to steer clear of the dreaded Land of the Helpers. The ground they were traveling on in this part of Mangonel was soft and dry. It was like walking on dry sand covered with a blanket. The area was filled with bushes and shrubs no more than three feet high. The space between the plants was unencumbered. Farther east, the terrain changed. The bushes were being crowded out by a multitude of moss-covered rocks. The existence of so much moss was a mystery, because there was no indication of sufficient moisture here to support the profusion of moss. The question was, if there was enough water to allow so much moss, there should have been enough water for the bushes to grow much larger than the stubby plants that existed here.

As the plant-life became scarce, the stones became more prominent. Not only were there more of them, they were bigger. Continuing east, the stones choked out the plants. The stones increased in size until they were boulders weighing many tons. The entire area was crowded with boulders, creating a mazelike configuration, and some confusion for the travelers. They continued walking through the giant rocks until they eventually realized they had, in fact, unknowingly entered a boulder maze. This produced a new problem: how to get back out.

Taking one turn or another without a plan would have quickly led them to one dead end after another. Luckily, experience with this sort of thing made their escape much easier than it might have been. Buddy started marking the stones at each turn to show where they had been. Pesky, on the other hand, decided they could cover much more ground if they split up.

At one intersection Pesky disappeared down an alleyway before Sly or Buddy could stop him. His impatience led him down one path until he came across another intersection. He would then randomly pick a direction and head off again.

This process did nothing but get him lost. Finally, reaching a dead end, Pesky turned around and headed back toward the others. At the first crossroad he came to, he realized his mistake. He had no way of knowing how to get back to his friends. The boulders were slick and tall, so he was unable to climb on top to see where he was. Without a clue regarding his whereabouts, or what he was supposed to do next, Pesky sat down and cried.

Meanwhile, Buddy and Sly were frantically searching for their friend. They didn't separate company. They correctly figured that going different ways would just cause all of them to get lost. Fearfully, they scurried in and out of passages while they marked their passing. Up and down the paths, in and out of dead ends they went, all the while calling Pesky's name. Then, during a pause in their calling, they heard Pesky calling back, "Over here, I'm over here." Even though they could hear him, they had no idea how to reach him. The maze was large, with many twists, turns, and dead ends. The boulders caused an echo that made it impossible to tell where Pesky's voice was coming from. It sounded like it was coming from several directions at once.

Eventually they stepped into an intersection, and there sat Pesky. He was so frightened he was shaking from head to tail. "I am so sorry. I thought I was helping, but all I did was cause more trouble."

Sly stepped over to Pesky, and gave him a hug. She assured him that all was fine, and that they were just happy to have found him. After being reunited with his pals, Pesky didn't say a word. He stayed in the back, following Sly and Buddy through the maze.

Even though they spent hours meandering through the boulders, it didn't seem very long to Buddy or Sly. They looked at the experience as one more obstacle to overcome, one more challenge, one more puzzle to solve, one more adventure. They were actually having a good time. Pesky, on the other hand, was miserable. He was having a hard time forgiving himself. Buddy had to take him aside and talk to him. In hushed tones he told the little raccoon, "Don't fret so. If you hadn't gone off without us, we would still be searching that area of the maze, and we would have been stuck in here that much longer. Actually you were a big help." Then in a hushed whisper he said, "But for our sake, don't run off again. One more thing—I almost went out on my own too. Don't tell Sly; it will just upset her."

With that little secret between them, Pesky felt much better. He even began to make suggestions. At one corner he hinted they take the right leg rather than the left. It really didn't matter to Buddy, and if it would bring Pesky back to his old self, why not go that way? Two more corners, taking a left, then a right, and they burst out of the maze. Pesky was so proud that he had helped find the way out he ran right up Buddy's back, and danced on his head. "What a pesky little raccoon," Buddy commented, and they began to laugh.

When the excitement died down, they gazed about. Around two hundred yards in front of them, two football field lengths away, they saw a group of tall men working to break the boulders into pieces. These men were not like other men. Buddy and his group could almost see through them. Each man was a perfect specimen of the human male, with muscles aplenty. All of them looked like statues the early Romans carved from marble, but these men were not made of marble, and they could move. They were nearly transparent, but they varied in color from pale yellow to dusty brown. Each consisted of one large stone carved perfectly into the form of a man. With the exception of the color variations, and the features on their faces, they were identical.

As they approached, one of the sculptured men noticed the three strangers and stopped his work. Soon the others stopped as well. Each man turned to face the new arrivals. Buddy had noticed that although they were breaking boulders into small rocks, none of them held a tool. There were no hammers, no chisels, and no cutting tools of any sort. *How can that be?* he thought.

"Good afternoon," Sly shouted as they got closer. "I am Sly." As she pointed to the other two standing next to her, she said, "This is Pesky, and the big fellow is Buddy, our leader." That was a shock to Buddy. He never saw himself as the leader. They were all in this together.

One of the men stepped forward and spoke to the three strangers with a grating voice. He sounded like he was rubbing fingernails across a chalkboard when he spoke. It was irritating from the start. Gazing down on the three travelers, he asked, "How did you find your way through the boulder maze? We have been trying for centuries. Since we could find no way out, we began breaking all the boulders into pieces in the hope that someday we would reach the other side."

Pesky, never very diplomatic, asked, "How did you get here in the first place? What are you?"

"Good questions. Do you know Zandordrake?"

Buddy nodded. "We know of him."

"He molded us to keep him company, but he never gave us names. We are collectively known as the Lonsdaleites. We were made from a mineral called lonsdaleite. Lonsdaleite is very rare in its natural state. It's formed when a meteorite containing graphite hits the earth. Zandordrake was able to magically produce the right amount of heat and pressure to large amounts of graphite he had conjured up. From the stones he created, he made us, the men you see before you. We are constructed of the hardest rock known to man, many times stronger than diamonds."

So that is why they are able to break the boulders with their fists, thought Buddy.

"Zandordrake became bored with us. He disliked our voices so much he abandoned us here, trapped between the Forbidden Zone and that boulder maze behind you."

"The great wizard made it impossible for us to find an exit, but you were able to find your way in here; do you think you could help us find a way out?"

In Buddy's mind, Zandordrake had done the unthinkable, imprisoning these men behind a boulder maze. These creatures of magic had been trapped for centuries. They had no way of escaping because of the forces of a magical barrier. Buddy wanted to help them, so he started to think of his own situation. *No water, no food, no shelter, the unknown territory of the Forbidden Zone ahead of us, and the boulder maze behind,* he thought. Buddy suggested a respite before they headed out of the maze and on to the next leg of their adventure. He sat and pondered his alternatives. *We will not risk the Forbidden Zone. We'll go back through the maze. After all, no one knows what is in the Forbidden Zone. It is forbidden to go there, and someone named it that for a reason. There is no need to take any wild chances.*

Having made up his mind, Buddy spoke to his friends. "We're going through the maze again. We'll need a new set of marking symbols during our search for an exit," he announced. Calling the stone men close, he said, "Since we three will be leaving, all you Lonsdaleites need to do is follow us."

"What will you do when you escape?" Sly asked one of the stone men with a yellow hew.

"We have no need to do anything. We are stones. We don't eat or drink; we just work until dark, rest at night, even though there is no need, and start again in the morning. As rocks you can imagine our patience, but even we are growing tired of this."

While they rested, Buddy and Sly agreed on a new set of markings to be placed on the walls of the maze so they wouldn't be confused with the ones they made coming in. Once that was established, they told the stone men they were prepared to leave.

Entering the maze for a second time, they forged ahead, marking boulder after boulder until they came to a dead end. They would then retrace their steps and search another corridor. It was a long and tedious process, with little progress, but as time passed they eliminated many passages.

Along their way, they found stranded stone men who had gotten lost in the maze. These men joined the parade that was attempting to solve the puzzle of how to get out. Again, it took numerous hours of searching; however, rather than wandering aimlessly about, they had a pattern, a plan, and that made all the difference in the world.

Buddy was leading the group when he made a turn and stepped into a large field of grass. Everyone was as surprised, and as pleased as they could be, until someone repeated the question regarding what the stone men would do now that they were free.

It didn't take them long to realize they were facing a future without anything to keep them busy, not even breaking boulders. Sly, always thinking, offered this solution. "Why don't you go over to the Land of the Helpers and see if they want their dirt roads paved in stone? The farmers in the volcano could use some exit roads, and maybe you could convince them to leave that dangerous place. I know Good King Garondrake could use your help in getting his stone castle repaired. There will be plenty work for you, if you search for it."

This was such a good idea that the Lonsdaleite men all cheered aloud, nearly causing the others to go deaf. Buddy pointed out which direction the Lonsdaleites should go. Without a word of thanks, the stone men began to walk off. Sly said it was fine that they didn't offer any thanks. After all, they were made of stone, and they had had little interaction with other people, so they didn't know how to act.

Facing east, standing side by side, Buddy, Sly, and Pesky started walking down the small path before them. When the path began to press in on both sides of the travelers, Sly took the lead, followed by Pesky, and Buddy brought up the rear. Suddenly, Sly vanished. Pesky and Buddy stopped dead in their tracks. "What just happened?" shrieked Pesky.

Buddy pulled his little friend back as he moved to the front. Gingerly taking another step forward, he watched as his foot disappeared. A brief moment later, he felt something grab his leg and pull on it. He yanked himself free of the invisible grip, but he couldn't pull his foot back into view. The thing grabbed him again, and yanked harder. Unprepared for the force being put against his invisible foot, and unable to stand very long on the foot he could see, Buddy fell. He tried to gain his balance, but lost it and toppled forward instead of backward. This put his head near his previously absent foot. Looking up, he saw Sly still pulling him to her. Buddy looked back and saw half his body was missing. This had to be another mysterious gate in Mangonel. Before he went any further through the gate, he motioned for Pesky to follow him. Then, he pulled himself upright, and disappeared completely from Pesky's sight.

All of his friends were gone. But he had the assurance from Buddy that if he followed, everything would be fine. Pesky took a deep breath, closed his eyes, and walked down the path. When he opened his eyes, he was standing toe to toe with Buddy, who was looking down at him with a wide grin.

Sly told them they couldn't return to the Boulder Maze on this path. The gate they had just passed through only went in one direction, away from the maze, not to it. Buddy thought of the stone men again and wished them good luck in the future.

"Okay," said Buddy, as he pulled the map from his bag. "Let's see where we are. Maybe the map will give us a hint to what is at the end of this path."

Dictionary—Chapter 20

Abandoned: *Left alone without being cared for or supported*

Aimlessly: *Without purpose or direction*

Alleyway: *A passage, usually between two buildings*

Caldera: *A large crater in a volcano caused by an eruption*

Century: *One century is one hundred years*

Conjure: *To perform a magic trick*

Convince: *To persuade someone to do something*

Diplomacy: *A skill in dealing with people in a proper and acceptable manner*

Dormant: *Temporarily inactive*

Eliminate: *Permanently remove something*

Established: *Recognized as true*

Exception: *Something or someone not included*

Forged: *To make something with great effort and through the use of very high heat*

Frantic: *Out of control*

Fret: *To worry*

Gingerly: *Very cautiously*

Graphite: *A soft, dark carbon. Pencil leads are made of this*

Grating: *Rough and annoying sound*

Identical: *Exactly the same*

Impending: *Something about to happen*

Impression: *What stays in somebody's mind*

Impossible: *Too difficult. A problem without a solution*

Irritating: *Annoying*

Miserable: *Feeling very unhappy*

Multitude: *A large number*

Pattern: *A design, a model to be used as a guide*

Patience: *An ability to wait for long periods while staying calm*

Profusion: *Having a lot of something*

Prominent: *Well known, noticeable, sticking out*

Realize: *To know and understand something*

Respite: *A short rest*

Scarce: *Not enough or rarely found*

Scattered: *In a number of different places and away from each other*

Scurried: *Moved fast*

Sufficient: *Enough, as much as is needed*

Tedious: *Boring because it is too long, monotonous, or repetitive*

Transparent: *Able to be seen through*

Unencumbered: *Without responsibilities or problems*

Vanished: *Walked on, across, or over something*

Variations: *Items of the same type, size, weight, etc., but with slight differences*

CHAPTER 21

I-Mees

Buddy and his two companions had just left the Lonsdaleite Stone Men and the Boulder Maze when they stumbled upon yet another gate within the kingdom of Mangonel. This particular gate went in only one direction, and of all things, it was invisible. Turning to continue down the path that led away from the invisible porthole, they discovered they were not far from an entrance to a village they had not seen before. There was an arched entrance that crossed over the path they were traveling. A sign etched in the arch read, "Welcome to I-Mees." Buddy, recalling some of his more unpleasant encounters, shuddered. He hesitated before passing under the arch. Even the name of this place gave him goose bumps. He had a nagging feeling that if he went under the arch, there would be trouble. He had a premonition—a sense that something was not quite right with this place. It was very much like the feelings Sly and Pesky had when they were about to go into the community of Volcano Farmers. Buddy wasn't one to look for trouble; enough came his way without searching for it, but he felt it coming in this village.

Sly and Pesky were right on Buddy's heels, almost pushing him while they tried to convince him everything would be fine. His friends were itching to go into the village. They were ready to go for several reasons. They were looking forward to another adventure; they were tired of camping out on the road; and they were eager to meet some new people.

Eventually, Buddy gave in. He stepped under the arch and into the village. They walked with cautious purpose, looking left and right, examining the village as they went. Every house had hexagonal doors, and oval windows. Every house was painted white; every door was painted red; and every window frame was painted blue. As the people came out of their homes, Buddy, and his friends noticed they all wore the same color clothes. Every person's outfit was only slightly different in design.

After advancing further into the village, and having reached an intersection of six different roads, Pesky turned around to make sure there was a way to get out. He was looking for an escape route. This was an old habit from birth. He inherited an abundance of curiosity; and curiosity generally got him into situations requiring some sort of escape. Pesky grabbed Buddy by the leg to stop him; then he asked, "If you spin around, and try to remember which road we came in on, can you find it? I can't."

Buddy and Sly both turned slowly, looking down each of the six roads. When they stopped, they had already become confused. Every road had the same type of houses, all painted the same. There was no telling which road they entered on. They had just arrived, and already they were lost. Buddy thought to himself, *I knew it; I just knew there was going to be trouble.* Instead of saying what he was thinking, Buddy snorted in a tone that meant business, "Pick one of the roads; we're leaving. As we go, we'll make some marks at the intersections, just like we did in the boulder maze. One of these roads leads out. There are only six, and we didn't come into this town all that far."

Sly picked up a stone and marked the dirt near the side of the road so passersby wouldn't disturb it. As soon as she did this, one of the villagers came running up and erased the mark, shouting, "You can't do that. You don't have permission. You'll get in serious trouble if you try to do something without permission. If the Boss Lady doesn't allow it, you don't do it." The guy, all dressed in purple, stood with his arms akimbo waiting for an answer. When he got none, he stammered, "Wha … Who are you three? Why aren't you dressed in purple? Are you trying to get the Boss Lady angry?" While this was happening, many more of the citizens gathered near the intersection.

Before the man could say anything more, a woman approached from one of the six roadways. She was not very tall, maybe five and one half feet tall. She was shapely and attractive, well dressed in a long purple dress that hugged her upper body to her waist, and then flared out as it reached her ankles. A high collar hid her slender neck and looked as if it might be too tight. The entire deep purple outfit accented her long, flowing blond hair. For a woman her age, she had a cute face; not elegant, not excessively pretty, but young looking. Her cute face belied her nasty attitude. The woman's voice didn't match her appearance either. Her tone and manner were all authoritative. She was gruff and rude.

"What's going on here?" She looked at the frightened citizen as she spoke, acting like Buddy, Sly, and Pesky weren't even there. "Speak up, Andrew," she demanded. "Don't just stand there like some silly frog."

When the Boss Lady arrived, all the others who were beginning to gather quickly disappeared into their nearby homes. Hidden in their houses, they peered out their windows to see what was going to happen next. Andrew felt less pressure without all the people gathered around, but it was clear he was still afraid of the Boss Lady. It was apparent he didn't want to offend the woman by saying the wrong thing. Andrew chose his words carefully. "I found these three wandering the streets. I followed them to see what they were up to. They stopped here before deciding to go on, and when they started up the street again, they made a mark in the road." He quickly added, "The mark is gone; I already cleaned it up."

Knowing she was going to get no more information from Andrew, the Boss Lady turned to the new arrivals. "Well, what have you to say for yourselves? How dare you come into *my* village and mark up *my* beautiful roads? Did you speak to anyone? Did you say something to this—frogish man? When you are in *my* village, you speak to *me*," she demanded.

All three stood in shock and had no reply to such demands. Sly was the first to come to her senses and offered a response. "We are weary adventurers who have traveled to many places in the kingdom of Mangonel. We stumbled across this village and—"

"*This* village?" interrupted the lady. "*This* village, you say? I will have you know this is **MY** village."

"And may we inquire your name?" asked Sly.

Calming down, the woman presented herself to the visitors. "My name is Janet, Janet E. Gotist, and as I said, this is *my* village. Everything belongs to *me*. *I* control everything around here. If *I* don't have something that I want, I demand that I get it, and these underlings of mine get it for me. When *I* say to wear green or gray, blue or yellow, the whole village does as I say. *I* am the Boss Lady in *my* village."

Buddy finally shook his head to remove the shock that was keeping him from saying anything. "Okay, if this is your village, and your name is Janet, then why did you name the village 'I-Mees'?"

"It is a ridiculous occurrence with a simple explanation," the Boss Lady responded with a haughty air. "I arrived here years ago in this place they called 'Plain Borough.' Can you imagine? Anyway, as I was saying, after I arrived, I found a family who took me in. They weren't able to give me all I wanted, so I hounded them until they decided to leave their home, thereby giving it to *me*. Everyone here is like this cowering—frog-man. They were afraid to challenge me, so I appointed *myself* as the Boss Lady. I wanted a new name for *my* village, but I just couldn't decide. I heard these—these people whispering as I passed by, and a great deal were saying something about I and me. They said it so often I decided to name the village after them, the I-Mees." She uttered a nasty little snicker. Janet was so impressed with herself; she didn't see the irony in this. She thought it a joke and an insult to the people. She didn't understand it was a reflection of her own selfishness.

Janet E. Gotist stood as tall as she could while waiting for one of the three strangers to say something. Pesky said under his breath, "Should have named the village after her and called it Egotist." Sly and Buddy couldn't hold the giggles in.

Janet, the Boss Lady, grew very angry. "*I* don't like your laughing. Are you laughing at *me*? Stop it, you hear? Stop I say! This is *my* village, and everyone does *my* bidding. When you entered this village, you became *my* property. You belong to *me*, and you will do as I say."

Buddy and Sly and Pesky laughed harder with each word she said. That was, until she said they were her property. The laughter stopped then. Janet thought they were obeying her. "That's much better. Now you will go to the seamstress and have her make you a set of purple clothes for the day. Be off! I don't want to look at you until you are properly attired."

Buddy had had about all he was going to take from this Boss Lady. It was his turn to stand up tall. You could hear the air being sucked in from all the people even though they were far away and still hiding inside their houses. He took in a deep breath of his own to calm himself down. Then he began. "Okay, lady! You may have bullied all these people, but you will not bully me or my friends. We are visitors, but that doesn't mean you can treat us like we belong to you. You want us to leave? Fine, we will go. Just point out the road we came in on, and we'll be on our way."

Pesky then shouted at the top of his lungs, "*Your* village is boring. Making everyone follow your rules, giving them no choice, you've made this village dull and boring. You and all your orders to have every house built and painted the same, and all the people dressed the same, *yuck*!" He turned to Andrew, "Do you like your village this way?"

Suddenly, Andrew wasn't so afraid. He had seen someone stand up to the Boss Lady, even a tiny raccoon. He knew he too could stand up to her, now that he had gathered the courage. Andrew swallowed hard, looked Janet right in the eye, and said, "No, I don't like my village to be like this. I think we all want some say in how the village looks. We want some individuality."

Janet E. Gotist couldn't believe what was happening. "Just who do you think you are?" she shouted at Andrew.

"I'm not a frog; I can tell you that. And all these people are not sheep." Many people had gathered around by now, and they were all nodding their heads in agreement. "Today I'm going to change my clothes and begin to paint my house the way *I* want."

Some of the others, softly at first, and then much louder, began to say, "Me too. I want a blue house with white shutters." Another chimed in, "I always wanted a tan house with turquoise trim around the doors and windows." It didn't take long before everyone was shouting out the new colors they were going to paint their homes.

The Boss Lady realized she had lost all control. The people of her village were not hers to command anymore. At first she was angry. Her blood boiled as the crowd continued to shout how they were going to change things. Then she became less and less angry and a little more ashamed. The crowd simmered down. They were all staring at Janet.

Sly felt sorry for her, so she called out a suggestion. "I think Janet can see she was too bossy, but can't you see how nice and clean your village is? There doesn't appear to be any crime here, and you all have water and food. I think these are all signs of a good leader, don't you?"

Not many agreed with Sly, but a few did. Sly then offered, "Andrew was the first to speak out about Janet's bossiness, so I suggest he be your new leader. Perhaps Janet could help him with all the good ideas she has." Everyone began chanting, "Andrew, Andrew, Andrew."

Buddy had something to add. He looked at Andrew and Janet. His enormous size commanded attention. "I don't want to be like Janet, so I won't tell you what to do. However, like Sly suggested, I too think Andrew, the former frog-man, should be your new leader. I also think he could use Janet's help to run the town. Together they ought to be able to lead you well." Soon, the majority of the town agreed they would give Andrew and Janet a try.

"We wish we could stay and assist you in rebuilding your village," said Buddy, "but we will be leaving in the morning." He stared into the eyes of Andrew and Janet. "If you continue to run this village in the same manner you have been, well, then you deserve to live in a dull and boring place."

Andrew then offered to have the three travelers spend the night with him. After a short period of contemplation, he looked at Janet. "Since we have a lot of planning to do together, we might as well start right away. Why don't you join us for dinner?" And Janet accepted.

Dictionary—Chapter 21

Abundance: *A large amount of something*

Accented: *Marked with a particular pronunciation or emphasis*

Advancing: *Moving forward or ahead*

Agreement: *To see things in the same way*

Akimbo: *To bend elbows outward and rest the hands on the hips*

Apparent: *Clearly understood*

Appointed: *Assigned*

Arched: *A semicircular opening for passage*

Ashamed: *Embarrassed for doing something wrong or unkind*

Attired: *Clothed*

Audience: *People watching or listening to a performance, show, or speech*

Authoritative: *Reliable, the trait of showing others you are in charge*

Belied: *To give a false impression*

Bullied: *Aggressive and intimidating*

Challenge: *To dare someone*

Chime in: *To speak*

Contemplation: *To think hard on something*

Convince: *To make certain and persuade someone to do something*

Courage: *Brave*

Cowering: *Cringe or shake in fear of something or somebody*

Egotist: *Someone with too high of an opinion of himself or herself*

Elegant: *Good taste in appearance and behavior*

Enormous: *Unusually large*

Etch: *To cut a design into something*

Gather: *To form into a group*

Gruff: *Abrupt and angry in manner or speech, harsh sounding*

Haughty: *Behaving in a superior way*

Hesitated: *Held back, waited for a short time before going on, slow to act*

Hexagonal: *Having six sides*

Hounded: *To follow, chase, or pester someone without ever letting up*

Identify: *To recognize somebody or something*

Individual: *A single person or entity that is different from the group*

Inherit: *To be given something from the time of your birth*

Intersection: *A crossroad, a crossing point*

Insult: *To be offensive to another person*

Interrupt: *To halt a speaker from talking by talking over him or her*

Irony: *Something thought to be funny based on words that suggest the opposite of their real meaning*

Occurrence: *A happening*

Offend: *Cause somebody to be angry or hurt*

Passerby: *Somebody going past another person or place*

Peer: *To look at something carefully, especially when it is hard to see*

Permission: *To allow something to be done*

Purpose: *The reason for existence*

Reflection: *Careful thought, especially when considering previous actions. Also a duplicate image on a shiny surface*

Response: *A reply or answer to a question or statement*

Ridiculous: *Silly to the point of being unreasonable and nonsensible*

Rude: *Ill-mannered*

Seamstress: *A woman who is an expert at sewing; a man is called a tailor*

Senses: *The ability to make intelligent decisions and wise judgments*

Simmer: *Cooking at just below boiling.*

Smirk: *A disrespectful smile*

Stammered: *To speak with hesitation and repeated syllables or consonants*

Turquoise: *A greenish blue color*

Underlings: *People who are looked upon as a lesser class and to be used*

Weary: *Tired*

CHAPTER 22

Hairy Feud

The people in the village of I-Mees were a strange lot. Buddy and his pals were glad to leave them behind. The overbearing leader, Janet E. Gotist, had promised to give up her old ways. She agreed to work together with the people, and by the looks of things, the whole place was about to experience a complete makeover. With Andrew as the new leader in the village and the organizational skills of Janet, they were going to do fine. All the people seemed happy with the proposed alterations in leadership. Their new freedoms to dress the way they wanted and their right to paint their houses the colors they liked were a big success.

The morning they left I-Mees, it was dark and gray. The sky threatened to send a downpour on the travelers. None of this dampened the spirits of the threesome as they ambled along without a care to weather or to where the road was leading. They were happy to be traveling with their best friends, and to them, in spite of the gloom, the day was gorgeous. It seems that no matter how dreary a day may appear, good friends and a good attitude can turn it into a pleasant one.

Buddy, the tallest of the group, was first to spot the figure approaching them on their path. As they closed the distance between themselves and the other traveler, they could see he was alone and enjoying the morning as much as they were. He was average in height and build, but that was where all familiarities stopped. His hair was cut short on one side, and long on the other. His clothes were equally strange. One side was dressed like a pauper, with his clothes all torn, ragged, and dirty. The side, where his hair was cut short, was adorned in fancy dress clothes. The whole ensemble was silly looking. He wore only half of every garment. His left side was clothed in a starched white shirt, red tie, black suit with a vest, a fancy belt and a highly polished shoe. The right side was covered in a dirty, torn T-shirt, tattered jeans and a frayed, untied sneaker.

The man stopped dead in his tracks. With a big smile on his face, he announced, "What is forever evil combined with a round exclamation?"

No one spoke. They remained dumfounded by the man's strange attire, and equally befuddled with his strange talk.

"Come on, come on! Under the circumstances that is an easy one."

Again, everyone was silent. Eventually, Pesky broke the silence with a greeting. "Hello."

"Exactly," the man nearly yelled. "I must say that was very good—very good indeed! You others still seem lost, so I'll explain. You see, 'forever evil' is *hell*, and the 'round exclamation' naturally refers to *oh*. Combining the two, as the riddle suggests, is equivalent to saying *hello*."

Pesky had not gotten it at all. He had merely stumbled upon the answer when he stated his greeting.

Buddy spoke next. "We are Buddy, Sly, and Pesky. Who are you? Can you tell us what lies ahead?"

"As to what lies ahead is a battle so kind, nobody gets hurt, but there is no change of mind. As to who I am, I am the Traveling Riddler. I love to make riddles about everything. Let me try another easy one on you. What has twelve legs and three brains but can't solve a riddle for beans?"

Sly responded to that one. "If your intention is to impress us with your riddle, you have not succeeded, but if you intend to ridicule us instead, you have accomplished your goal. I have solved your riddle; you are speaking of the three of us, and I don't care for the implication."

The man's smile broadened as he tossed out one more riddle and began walking away. "Who can make you think, and try to find the link, while he disappears in a blink?"

Buddy solved that one, and shouted the answer after the man. "*You*," he called.

"Bravo, now you're getting it."

"Is it me, or did you guys think that guy was bizarre too?" asked Pesky. "And what do you think he meant by, 'a battle so kind, nobody gets hurt, but there is no change of mind'?"

"I'm not sure," replied Buddy, "but it doesn't sound too bad." He paused. Looking up the path he added, "Let's go see."

Late in the afternoon the path they were traveling on was obstructed by a fence. It wasn't a high fence, and it wasn't very secure. It was made of six-foot-high posts and only three rails from top to bottom. Anyone could easily crawl under it, through it, or over it. The barricade was so easy to penetrate it seemed to have no purpose. The traveling trio decided it might be best to walk along the outside of the barrier to see if they could get an idea what was happening on the other side.

At one point, they came across another connecting fence that ran perpendicular to the one they were following. Attached to both sides of this new boundary line were signs, each written in a different manner, but each one announced the same sort of warning: "*No trespassing. Stay on your own side of the fence.*"

Sly read the signs out loud to the others and then turned to face them. "I believe this oddity bears looking into. Shall we cross this ridiculous obstacle and follow the new course?"

Buddy and Pesky were more than up for the challenge. Before Sly had said all she was going to say, Buddy was already climbing over the fence, while Pesky was going through the barricade that blocked their progress. The raccoon looked back at Sly and signaled her to hurry along. Buddy chose to travel on the west side of the new fence, while Sly traveled on the east. Pesky found it much easier to walk along the top rail.

Following the fence line that went in a northerly direction, they came across many signs placed on either side cautioning everyone not to cross. The signs said such things as: "*Stay out. Keep out. You are not welcome. Go away. Cross at own risk., Do not cross. Warning—leave now.*" This was not a very friendly set of neighbors.

Continuing along the fence, they came to a man on the west side of the divider. He seemed to be on the lookout for something. He was clad in a medieval tunic that resembled a uniform. He was dressed in a red and white tunic that was secured at the waist with a wide leather belt. He looked powerful, and his hair was very long. The hair was braided and reached all the way to his waist. The guard called out to them, "What manner is this? You travel both sides of the fence, and the middle at the same time. Who do you support, the Hairy clan or the Balders?"

Not knowing what the man was talking about, none of them had an answer. With mouths agape, all three stood silent.

The guard cupped his ear with his hand, "You three, stay here and make up your minds. I have a battle to go to." He turned briskly and ran along the edge of the fence.

"Did you hear anything?" asked Buddy. Neither Pesky nor Sly had heard a sound. Buddy started to follow the path the guard had taken and said, "Well, what are we waiting for? It's time to see what this is all about."

Just over the ridge they saw a raging battle going on. However, this battle was unlike anything they expected. People were gathered on either side of the fence. Some of the people on each side were collecting clods of dried mud, globs of sticky mud, handfuls of leaves, pine cones, acorns, mushrooms, and anything else that would do little or no harm. They carried these items to the front line where another group would snatch them up and hurl them one by one at the people on the opposite side of the fence.

At this time, Buddy, Sly, and Pesky got a better look at what was afoot. The people on the west side of the fence were friends of the fellow they had met. Everyone wore the same red and white uniforms and had long braided hair that hung down their backs. On the east side of the fence, everyone was bald. The bald people wore uniforms of blue and white, sewn in a pattern exactly opposite of the red and white uniforms of the hairy people.

It appeared the only way anyone was going to win was when one side ran out of soft things to throw or got too tired to throw anything. This had to be what the Traveling Riddler fellow was talking about, but it all made little sense to Buddy and his companions. They waited until, as they predicted, the tossing of things over the fence died down.

Sly couldn't hold herself back any longer. She nearly ran to the guard they had met earlier. "What is going on here? What manner of battle do you call this? What are you fighting about?"

The man looked as if no one had ever asked him these questions before, and perhaps no one had. The guard tried to explain. "You are all standing on the property of the Hairy Clan. Those rebels over there, with their heads all shaved, they're called the Balders. Years ago we were all one big happy clan. That was until some started to shave their heads. They disliked the long hair hanging down their backs. It was a rebellion against all we knew and against our ancestors, who all had long hair. We cast them out and built this fence to keep them out. It was a time-consuming and difficult job. Since they didn't want us crossing into their land any more than we wanted them over here, they helped us build the barrier. Now, whenever we see someone from the other side, we go to war in order to remind them to stay where they are."

Buddy was still confused. "So, this is nothing but a feud over the way you wear your hair? If you're really warring with one another, why do you only cast soft things?"

It was the guard's turn to look totally shocked. "Would you have us throw things that would hurt them? They're nice people, and they were once part of our clan. What kind of animals do you think we are? For that matter, what kind of animals are you?"

Sly continued, "May I suggest you call their leader to the fence for a powwow so we can discuss this?" The man did as she requested. A moment later the two leaders faced each other at the fence line.

Sly conducted the meeting. "Listen to me, you two. You were once a single clan. You liked each other so much you even combined your efforts to build this stupid fence. You obviously don't wish to hurt one another. Why not compromise and stop all this silliness?"

"And how do you intend for us to do that? What sort of compromise do you propose?" the two asked as one.

"I would first like to know with whom I am conversing. Please give me your names," began Sly.

The bald man spoke first. In a proud voice he announced that his name was Harry.

Then the Hairy guy, speaking even louder, stated his name. "And I am Baldwin."

"Oh, for Pete's sake. How ironic," Sly commented with a smile. "If I didn't see this myself, I would have never believed it."

Sly looked across the fence. "Harry, do you like being bald?"

"No, not really," said the leader.

"Would you mind growing your hair to your shoulders, half the length of the Hairy Clan?"

"No, I guess not. Actually being bald gets pretty cold sometimes."

"And you, Baldwin, do you think the Hairy Clan could meet the Balders halfway and cut their hair so it wouldn't grow past their shoulders?"

"That seems fair," said the guard dressed in red. "The extra-long hair is ridiculous anyway, and it's a pain to take care of."

"Fine," said Sly. "This is what I propose, and if you agree, you can tear down this fence and work together from now on. This side of the fence is to cut their hair to shoulder length, and that side of the fence is to let their hair grow to that same length. If you do that, you can be finished with all this ridiculous quarreling. Do you agree?"

The two men nodded their heads. "Wonderful," Sly continued. "Now shake hands, and get busy ripping down this barrier."

She looked up at Buddy and announced, "Well, another problem of Mangonel has been solved. Shall we depart for more exciting locations?"

"Sure," said Buddy. Pesky still didn't know what had happened. He stood there with his head sort of hanging to one side and his face all crunched up in a questioning manner as he waited for Buddy to lead them away.

Dictionary—Chapter 22

Accomplished: *Achieved a goal*

Adorn: *To add decorations to something*

Afoot: *About to happen*

Agape: *Wide open*

Alterations: *Changes*

Amble: *To walk slowly*

Approaching: *Drawing near*

Barricade: *A barrier, wall, or obstruction to protect the defenders of something*

Befuddled: *Confused*

Bizarre: *Amusingly or strangely unusual*

Braided: *Three or more strands interwoven without making a knot*

Briskly: *Done quickly*

Broaden: *To make something wider*

Clad: *Dressed*

Clods: *Clumps of dried dirt*

Challenge: *To invite someone to partake in a contest or fight*

Circumstances: *The conditions existing at a particular place and time*

Combined: *To put two or more things together*

Compromise: *To settle a dispute in which two or more sides agree to accept less than originally wanted*

Conduct: *Behavior*

Course: *Direction of travel*

Divider: *A device that separates one section from another*

Dumfounded: *So taken by surprise you are speechless*

Ensemble: *An entire outfit of clothing, including accessories*

Equivalent: *The same*

Exclamation: *A sudden cry of a word or phrase*

Feud: *A long dispute or quarrel*

Figure: *A human shape not seen very clearly*

Garment: *Clothing*

Gesture: *A sign or signal*

Gorgeous: *Beautiful*

Hurl: *To throw something*

Implication: *An indirect suggestion, a hint*

Impress: *Having a strong, usually a favorable effect on somebody's thinking*

Intention: *A planned meaning or purpose*

Ironic: *Involving a surprising and contradictory (opposite) fact*

Makeover: *A reshaping of someone's physical appearance or mental outlook*

Nonsense: *Senseless, pointless*

Obstruct: *To block something from happening or going forward*

Oddity: *Strange*

Organized: *An ability to keep things in order*

Pauper: *A person without any money*

Perpendicular: *At right angles to a line or plane*

Powwow: *To hold a meeting*

Predicted: *Stated the belief of a future happening or outcome*

Proposed: *Made a suggestion*

Raging: *Very strong*

Rebellion: *An uprising against something*

Rebel: *Somebody who rejects the codes and presently accepted practices*

Ridicule: *To mock or make fun of somebody in a hurtful way*

Ridiculous: *Silly and amusing*

Snatch: *To take away quickly*

Succeed: *Manage to do what was planned*

Trespassing: *To enter somebody else's land without permission*

MEDALLION OF MANGONEL

Mandrake?

What is the magic? How is this used?

The inscriptions make no sense; what is this? Snatched in a hurry.

CHAPTER 23

The Amazing Medallion

A feud over the length of someone's hair—what other ludicrousness would they come across in the days and weeks ahead? Even though some of Buddy, Sly, and Pesky's odd encounters were difficult to comprehend, and even more difficult to explain, they were all welcome adventures. Their most difficult time was traveling between one place and another. Although some interesting things did happen on occasion while traveling, most of the time it was just a long walk.

Pesky grew tired long before the other two. His legs were short, which made him akin to the farmers in the volcano who could only take small steps. He was forced to nearly run everywhere they went in order to keep up with the giant steps Buddy could take.

Walking for a few hours after leaving the Hairy people and the Balders, Pesky sat down and refused to go any further. "I'm tired of running all the time." Looking up at Buddy,

279

he declared, "One of you is going to have to carry me for a while."

The big bear didn't mind. The raccoon was small, and the provisions bag didn't weigh much, so the task of carrying Pesky would be easy. "Climb aboard, my little friend. I'll carry you for a time." With that, Pesky regained some of his energy and literally jumped onto Buddy's shoulders. Looking backward, all the raccoon could see was the provisions bag wrapped in the blanket as it dangled from its carrying stick. It gave the wily raccoon an idea. He leaned over and whispered into Buddy's ear, "What if the provisions bag has a map with the locations of all the gates in Mangonel? That could save us a whole lot of walking."

Now here was an idea worth exploring. He was surprised none of them had thought of it before. Perhaps Pesky didn't deserve to be called Pesky after all. No, he wasn't a pest; he was clever, much like Sly, and he was a loyal friend. Buddy called the troop to a halt, set the raccoon on the ground, and put the provisions bag in the center of the tiny circle they had formed. He then opened the sack, peered into the void before poking his hand inside, and stated his request. "I would like to have something that will show me where all the gates of Mangonel are located."

Within an instant something snapped into Buddy's hand. It was cold, hard, and round. It was disk shaped, not like a map at all. Slowly he removed the object from the bag. The disk he held was about six inches in diameter and attached to a chain. The chain and the disk were made of solid gold. The disk was made up of three circles, one solid circle in the center surrounded by two outer circles. A sliver of space separated the three so that the center circle could spin on an axis, like a top. The two outer circles could rotate, like clock hands. There were engravings on both sides of the object. Each marking was separated from the next by a straight line. It was obvious the lines were there to properly align the images.

Buddy realized he had made a mistake. Instead of asking for a map, he had asked for "something," and this is what he got. Now all they had to do was find out how to use it and decipher the meaning of the engraved symbols. That was not going to be so easy.

Sly took hold of the medallion and spun the center circle. There was only one symbol on either side. One side looked like a stylish letter M. The opposite side appeared to be two entwined letters. Closer examination of the second side gave the impression the letters were probably an L and a B. The whole thing looked magical and could have only been created by Zandordrake.

The outer circles had various markings. These engravings weren't letters; they were more like symbols. Each was beautiful. They were wonderful to look at, but none made any sense. None seemed to have a connection to another, and none matched. They were all distinctively different.

Sly held the medallion for a moment. She soon discovered when two markings were aligned at the top, where the chain was attached, none of the other lines matched. The lines that separated the marks were spaced in some special way so that no more than two symbols could be aligned at any time.

When they placed two markings at the top of the medallion they all expected some sort of reaction, but nothing happened. Buddy was relieved. He would have preferred to put the thing back in the bag. They had no idea how to read the markings on the medallion. Neither did they have any way of knowing what would happen when they figured out how to use it. They all suspected it would operate like one of the gates they had already experienced, but they weren't sure.

Buddy voiced his objections. "Let's get rid of this. I think we should put it back before it gets us into trouble."

Pesky was of another mind. "Where have we ever gone in Mangonel that we weren't able to take care of ourselves? If this is, as we requested, an instrument showing where the gates of Mangonel lie, and even if it is a gate itself, what is there for us to worry about?"

Sly agreed with this thinking, but there was still a problem. "I believe the chain was put there so someone could wear it around his or her neck. If the person wearing it is the only one who can use the medallion then it is of no use to us."

Buddy took the medallion by the chain and began to swing it around his arm. This gave him an idea, "If you two are really set on going through with this, I have an idea. We might not be able to get all of our heads through the chain, but we can each get an arm through it. Now, how do we make it work?"

They each put an arm through the chain, lined up two marks of the outer wheels, crossed their fingers for luck, and started giving directions to the medallion.

"Where to?" said Pesky.

"Show us the way!" called Sly.

"Which direction do we go?" shouted Buddy. Nothing happened. They tried everything they could think of, but the medallion did nothing and showed them nothing.

After a while they were all sitting on the ground with one arm each through the chain. Pesky wanted no more of the useless medallion and jokingly said, "Pleeeeease, take us to where the markings point."

Swish, in an instant they were transported to a place none of them had ever seen before. For a moment they were dizzy, but the effect quickly wore off. "It works," Pesky called out.

"Yes, my friend, the contraption seems to have conducted some sort of activity. Whatever it has done, it has included us in its journey. The medallion appears to be a transportation device, able to act much in the same manner as the gates we have encountered," concluded Sly. Looking around at the new terrain, she added, "Would you be so kind to enlighten us regarding our whereabouts?"

"What?" said Pesky with a furrowed brow. "How am I supposed to know that?"

Sly must have been very tired, and her next comment, though not harsh, still showed her frustrations. "You seem to have had all the answers thus far—at least all the answers that have gotten us into this place of who knows where. Tell us then, where are we?"

Buddy frowned at Sly. "That's not fair. We were all trying to make the medallion work. Pesky just happened to find the key. He has no more idea where we are than either of us." Buddy pulled out the map of Mangonel and searched the countryside for clues. It wasn't difficult to tell where they had landed. They were on an island, and everywhere they looked revealed nothing but more islands. It took just a glance at the map to see they had been deposited on one of the hundreds of clumps of land located in Island Maze Lake. "It looks like we are once again in the western region of Mangonel," he announced.

The island they had been transported to was small. In fact, it was so small Buddy could view the entire island when he stood up on his hind legs. There was nothing there, just sand. The tiny mound of dirt had absolutely nothing on it. There were no plants, no animals, no food, no wood, no vines, no people; nothing at all except the new arrivals, Buddy, Sly, and Pesky.

"Over there is a much bigger island, and there are trees and things growing on it," offered Pesky. "Hey, Buddy, do you think you could swim us over to that island? We could at least build another raft over there."

The big bear agreed this was a pretty good idea. He allowed his two friends to climb upon his back for the water crossing. Buddy comfortably stroked his way to the nearby shore. This island was populated by trees and other plants. There was one other thing on this piece of land that was missing on the one they had just left. Footprints were imprinted on the beach. This island was inhabited, but by whom?

A few steps through the trees brought them into a small wheat field that was alongside an even smaller corn patch. A number of other plants were interspersed throughout the corn stalks. Peas, carrots, cucumbers, celery, potatoes, and even strawberries were present. At the opposite side of the garden, they saw a few island-type shanties. The sides and roofs of the homes were made of grasses attached to pole frames. The outside walls had huge windows without glass panes, but there were overhanging grass awnings that were hinged at the top so they could be dropped down to cover the openings in case of bad weather.

The three visitors approached the buildings with care. As if by magic, all of the village inhabitants appeared in a circle around them. They were so quiet and quick in their arrival that none of the three even noticed them coming until they were already upon them.

"Um, hello," Buddy offered as an introduction.

"*Sssssshhhhhhhhh*!" came from every one of the island people.

"Why so quiet?" whispered the raccoon.

One old man stepped forward. His face and bare torso were deeply tanned, as were his bare legs that extended from shorts made from grass. His voice was as soft as a breeze. "You are on Whisper Island. Everything here must be done in hushed tones or complete silence."

Pesky, a bit softer this time, again asked, "Why?"

"Sorry to appear so rude. My name is Oscar Olderman. This island, and all the islands that are within Island Maze Lake, are subjected to the whims of the Water Wisp Imps. The little devils live in the lake. They are rarely seen as long as we keep quiet. When they hear noises they come out of the water to wreak havoc on everything. The last time they destroyed our crops. The time before that they pulled all the grass from our roofs. They may be small, tiny in fact, but there are hundreds and hundreds of them. There's no stopping them from doing whatever nasty deed they have in mind." The man looked around as if he expected imps to show up any second for speaking too loudly. "Please, just leave; go back from where you came before there is trouble."

"That's fine with us," blurted Sly. "How do we find our way out of this maze of islands?"

"The quickest way is to head due south and go from island to island in hop-scotch style. You want to stay out of the water as much as you can," said Oscar Olderman.

Pesky wanted to leave as soon as possible. "Great! Let's go," he said in his normal voice.

In seconds they were swarmed by scaly little imps. The devilish creatures were everywhere at once, crawling, running, and flying in all directions. They were tearing everything they could get their hands on into shreds. Buddy grabbed for them like he was fishing for them in a stream. After a few attempts, he caught one of the fancier ones. He held on to it in his strong fist. The little Water Wisp Imp screamed in anger. When she yelled out, it caused all the other imps to stop dead in their tracks.

"How dare you touch me," yelled the Imp. "I am never to be touched. Can't you see that I am Yevistina Meaniemost, queen of the Water Wisps? Unhand me, I say."

Buddy didn't loosen his grip one bit.

There was a long pause before the imp spoke again. "If you let me go, I'll grant you one wish." Buddy didn't move.

Another, even longer pause passed before the imp queen called out again, "All right! Two wishes, but no more."

Buddy let the time pass. After a moment of thinking, he said, "Okay, two wishes, and I will release you."

"All right, Queen Meaniemost, my first wish is that you no longer bother these good people on the islands of this lake, even if they make noise."

"Fine," said the queen with great reluctance. "What is your second wish?"

"My second wish is to be transported with my friends from this lake to the shore of the mainland, and without further interference from you or your people," stated Buddy.

"You drive a hard bargain, bear. All right, your wishes will be granted. Now let me go."

Since Sly had no way of testing the imp queen, she had no idea if the queen imp was telling the truth. This was the first imp Sly had ever seen. Quickly, before Buddy let the little creature go, Sly called out, "What happens if you don't grant the wishes?"

The queen gasped. "Not grant a promised wish … *not grant a promised wish*? Are you mad? The others would never believe me again. I would lose my powers. I would be banished from the lake. No one can be queen if they can't be trusted. You can be sure I will grant your wishes."

Buddy let the imp queen go free. She flew a few feet away, turned, waved her tiny hands in the air, and all the other imps dove back into the water. "So much for wish one. But you realize you didn't say we couldn't bother those along the edge of the lake," she said with a sneer. Then she flew around

Buddy, Sly, and Pesky five times as fast as she could while shouting odd syllables. "Oogob solibib alazin gamis kinkej delloffen iss landespin," she yelled.

The next instant Buddy and his pals were on the mainland looking back at the lake.

"That was interesting," commented Pesky. "I think we should get away from here as quickly as possible. We're on the mainland shore where the imps can be their nasty selves again. Should we try the medallion?"

Dictionary—Chapter 23

Akin: *Similar*

Align: *To place something in a straight line*

Awning: *An extended structure used to obtain shade over a door or window*

Banished: *Cast out. To send somebody away*

Comprehend: *To understand*

Conduct: *Acted in a certain manner*

Contraption: *A device or machine, especially one that is strange*

Decipher: *To figure out the meaning of something*

Deposit: *To set something down*

Diameter: *A straight line running from one side of a circle through the center and on to the other side of the circle*

Distinctively: *Uniquely characteristic to a person, group, or thing*

Encounters: *Come across or against something*

Engraved: *Cut or etched images into metal or stone*

Enlighten: *To give clarifying information to somebody*

Entwined: *Something that has been twisted together*

Hinged: *Jointed to provide moveable parts fastened to something, like a door or box*

Inhabit: *To live or occupy a particular place*

Imp: *A small, mischievous imaginary being*

Impression: *What stays in somebody's mind*

Imprinted: *A pattern or design or mark made by pressing something down onto something else*

Instrument: *An object intended for a specific use, a tool*

Interference: *Something blocking progress*

Intersperse: *To put or place something here and there among or in something else*

Jokingly: *Said or done with the intent of being funny, not serious*

Literally: *Taking and using the exact and most basic meaning*

Ludicrousness: *Foolishness*

Medallion: *A large decorative metal disk worn on a chain around the neck*

Objection: *A statement that shows that you disagree*

Occasion: *A particular time*

Overhanging: *To project over something, leaving a sheltered space underneath*

Populated: *An inhabited place*

Predicament: *A difficult or unpleasant situation*

Preferred: *To like or want something more than something else*

Realize: *To know and understand something*

Refuse: *Not accepting something*

Regain: *To get something back*

Relieve: *To end or lessen something unpleasant*

Reluctance: *A lack of enthusiasm or desire to do something*

Scaly: *Covered in scales, like a fish*

Shanty: *Small, crudely built shack or hut*

Sneer: *To show or express something with anger*

Stroke: *The complete movement of arms and legs when swimming*

Stylish: *Having good taste in what is fashionable*

Swarm: *Flying in a group*

Torso: *Upper body part*

Transport: *To carry someone or something from one place to another*

Troupe: *Group of travelers, usually performers*

Wily: *Cunning, shrewd*

CHAPTER 24

Rhyme

The medallion had proved to be useful, to a degree. Sure, it was capable of taking the person who wore it to any number of places in the kingdom of Mangonel, but without knowing what all the markings meant, there was no telling where they were going to wind up. The three adventurers had just escaped from what could have been a disastrous time with a bunch of Water Wisp Imps, not to mention a long trek through the maze of islands on Island Maze Lake. They were all happy to be gone from there.

Standing on the bank of the lake, Pesky suggested they take another shot at seeing where the medallion would send them. Buddy and Sly were more cautious. Just twisting and turning the dials with no idea what could happen next was to take unnecessary chances. However, Pesky was relentless.

"What's the big deal? Heck, we might go visit people we have already met or rediscover some of the places we have already seen. What would be so wrong with that? Look at the map.

According to what is shown, we have already been to many of the places indicated. It seems like the odds are in our favor. If nothing else, it sure beats walking," Pesky persisted.

His argument was logical, but Buddy was concerned there might be many more places on the map that were not shown, like the farmers who lived in the volcano. "I'm not sure that's such a good idea," Buddy remarked.

Sly was less apprehensive. "Nothing can be much worse than the Never-Ending Swamp, or the Dangerous Desert, and we got through those fine, and without the help of the medallion. I think no matter where we land, we have an immediate out with the pendant. Let's do it," She slipped her arm through the chain alongside of Pesky's.

Buddy relented at last. "Very well you two. Here we go," he said as he placed his arm amid the others. Buddy spun the middle disk. It stopped on "M" again. Sly turned the inner dial to a random marking. Pesky took his turn to align a marking on the outer circle with the one Sly had chosen. Buddy called to the medallion to perform its magical function. "Please take us to where the symbols point."

Instantly, they were whisked away into an open field with neatly scattered blocks of wood. There were hundreds of them in various sizes ranging from about one foot to the size of a house. Looking about, Buddy noticed a man sitting on top of one of the larger blocks. "All right, we're here. Let's go see who that fellow is over there and find out where 'here' is."

A short walk took them to the base of a huge piece of wood. The man atop the block stared down at them. He was taller than any man they had ever seen. He had to be over seven feet tall, and he was all muscle. His hair was cut short, with the top leveled off like a table. He wore no shirt, and he had a massive saw resting on his lap.

"Hello, hello, to you I say.
Whatever in the world has brought you this way?
You look like good fellows, so choose a block, take a rest.
You look a bit lost, so I'll help you my best," the man said with a smile and a wave of his free hand.

Buddy made the introductions, stating that they were adventurers traveling the kingdom with no particular destination. Then he asked the big man if he could tell them where they were and possibly explain all the perfectly square wooden blocks.

"I apologize for my omission.
I will explain, if you'll give your permission.
I am known as the woodsman, and called Big Ben;
Ask me twice and I'll tell you again.
The blocks that surround you are all square as can be.
They've been carved where they sit and have been carved by me.
This once was a forest, but the trees all fell down;
Branches and stumps all cluttered the ground.
I like things neat, and since nobody cared,

I cut all the stumps into these perfect squares." The man seemed pleased with his explanation and grinned widely.

"As to your location, the question you chimed,
You have entered my place, the land I call Rhyme."

All three sat on a wooden square gazing up at the man who could rhyme so easily.

"Here we go again. Another strange activity in Mangonel," mumbled Sly as a smile crossed her face. "Remember the gentleman who spoke with so many P words? It was annoying. I think this rhyme fellow isn't going to be much better."

Buddy answered, "I don't know, I sort of like it. I think I'll give it a try."

Buddy, gazing up at Ben, squinted in thought, and then called out to the tall gentleman sitting on top of the large block of wood.

"I can see why they call you 'Big,' Mr. Ben;
You are twice the size of most other men.
You've sawed these logs so nice and neat,
And they make for us a comfortable seat."
He looked at his partners. "Pretty good, huh!"
"Now, Mr. Ben, please could you tell,
Where we are in Mangonel?"

Another glance toward his friends. "I think I've got the hang of this." Sly and Pesky rolled their eyes in mock disgust.

"You are north and near the edge.
The Forbidden Lands are past that ledge.
You are safe if you go south, east, or west;
These are directions that will suit you the best.
Over that way is the Forest Fable.
You should go by there, if you are able.
As for me, I have not strayed far from this shelf,
So you must explore Mangonel all by yourself," said the big man.

Not getting much assistance from the giant, Sly pulled on Buddy's fur to get his attention. "Thank the man, rhyming if you must. We can leave here and inspect our map. This place will show up on the parchment now that we have been here."

"Fine, but I was having fun with the rhyming." Looking back at Ben, Buddy said,

"I'm afraid I must announce, my friend,
This conversation has come to an end.
Thanks for the rest; now we'll be on our way.

We hope to see you some other day." With that, they picked up their bag, faced the south, and began walking toward yet another adventure.

"Sorry you have to leave so soon.
Couldn't you stay until this afternoon?
I have yet to meet another rhyming one.
Our conversation has been so much fun.
I'm sure our friendship would grow much stronger,

If only you could stay a little while longer.
Maybe next time more rhymes we'll try,
but for now, 'tis only my sad good-bye," was Ben's last rhyme.

Buddy was unhappy to be leaving so quickly. He liked Big Ben and all his rhymes.

"Off we go with our bag, that's a fact.
Nobody knows if we'll ever be back," he teased.

"Good grief!" said Sly.

When Big Ben was out of sight, they stopped and pulled out their map. Sure as the sun shines, the land of Rhyme was indicated on the map. They now knew where they were, but they had no idea where they were going next. Then again, they really didn't care. By this time Buddy was getting more comfortable using the medallion. He pulled the chain from his neck and began swinging it in circles around his wrist. "Should we give this another try, or do you feel like walking for a while?"

The others smiled as they slipped their arms through the chain. Sly gazed up at her big bear friend and proposed Buddy have the honor of choosing where to go next. "This all started with you, my friend," she commented. "I do believe you should be the one to turn the dials to decide our next destination."

Buddy stared at the medallion until it became obvious he was uncomfortable deciding for all of them. "No, we are in this together; we will choose together, like we have been doing."

Each one took their turn manipulating the medallion. Buddy spun the center as he always did. This time the LB was facing him when it stopped. Sly and Pesky turned the outer circles to their chosen symbols. When all was set, they asked to be taken where the medallion indicated.

In a heartbeat they were transported to their new location. When they recovered from the medallion's effects, they were in shock. They had never been to such a dismal place. All of the trees were dead and black with soot. The ground was dark gray with black puddles scattered about. Nothing had any color. Even the sky was brown. To one side, a forest of devastation loomed in ominous dreariness, and in back of them there was a sheer cliff that rose several hundred feet in the air. The cliff face was nearly smooth and impossible to climb.

Sly was the first to voice her concerns. "I don't know about you, but I have this awful, overwhelming sense of doom. I think we should go no farther." The others agreed almost immediately.

Near the cliff face there was a sign posted on one of the trees. Buddy led the group over to the board to see what it said. The sign looked like it had been written by several people, each one taking a finger and scribbling their message in black charcoal rubbed from the tree. The letters warned, "*Leave now!*" Below that it read, "*Get out while you can,*" and the most disturbing message of all: "*Beware! You have entered the Land Beyond. Go back before it's too late.*"

"The Land Beyond," remarked Buddy. "I know what the innermost circle on the medallion does. The M on one side designates places in the kingdom of Mangonel, and the LB on the other side designates places in the Land Beyond. We're lucky we arrived near this sign. I suggest we heed the warnings and use the services of the medallion to get out of here as quickly as possible."

Neither Sly nor Pesky wanted to argue the point. Buddy wound the medallion's chain around their arms and spun the inner circle. This time it stopped perpendicular to the other rings, not landing on M or LB. Pesky turned the inner circle to a symbol that appeared to have been all scratched over, as if someone had tried to remove it. Sly decided to match the scratched-out mark on the outer circle to coincide with the one Pesky had picked. These symbols obviously were meant to go together. "It looks as though these two markings may have been a mistake, or they were carefully marred to show they go together. Wherever this takes us ought to be interesting." she said. Then, before there could be any adjustments, she called out, "Please take us to where these symbols point."

True to form, the medallion performed exactly as it had in the past. In an instant they were whisked away. However, this time Buddy felt dazed as well as dizzy. He was also somewhat confused. Looking around to see where he was, he saw they were surrounded by drooping branches and leaves that made Buddy feel like he was inside a leafy igloo. Straight in front of him he saw Sly sniffing the ground for something, and Pesky was to his right with his nose in the provisions bag. "Pesky," he called out, "get out of there." Before he had finished what he was saying, Pesky looked up in shock, turned around, and ran through the leaves. At the same time, Buddy could see Sly dart out through the leaves from where she stood.

Buddy glanced at the provisions bag; it was different. It looked more like a backpack than the provisions bag. It also had something marked on it. It had a castle drawn on the back. When he reached for the bag, he saw his paws were gone; he now had hands. The bush, when he first shook the cobwebs from his mind, seemed to be normal, but now he noticed the black and white leaves. He was home again. At last he was back on earth, and in Colorado, his home.

Gathering up his book and backpack, he nearly ran all the way home. The day had passed, and although it wasn't dark yet, it was nearing dinner time. His mother would be home waiting for him, and he didn't want her to worry any more than she already had.

Buddy burst through the kitchen door to find his mother preparing dinner at the counter. He ran to her and hugged her tightly. "Mom, you won't believe what happened to me in the park today." He took a step back and began telling her everything from the moment he left the house until he entered the kitchen again. His mother listened with a limited amount of interest. When Buddy had finished, she remarked, "What a great day for you, Buddy. I am so happy you had such a wonderful adventure. You have the most interesting imagination. Now go wash up for supper."

Buddy felt a little down in the dumps. His mother's attitude made him understand. It was all just his imagination. He went to his room and began to sort out the truth of it. He had fallen asleep. While sleeping he had had the most vivid and amazing dream ever. He removed the uneaten snacks from his pack and tossed the bag to its normal resting place in the corner of his room by the closet. There was a clink when it hit the floor. Buddy couldn't fathom what might still be in the bag. He went and lifted the pack again. He shook it, and sure enough, there was something inside.

Taking the backpack to his bed, he turned it upside down. A soft thud on the blankets told him the hidden item had fallen free. Peeking around the backpack to get a glimpse at what had come from his pack, his chin nearly hit the floor. There, nestled in the folds of his blanket, was a gold medallion attached to a heavy gold chain. He lifted the object to inspect it further. It had a center circle with two outer circles. The inner circle had an M on one side and LB on the other. Buddy nearly fainted; it was the magical medallion from the kingdom of Mangonel.

Buddy's shock was tempered by his curiosity. Why had the medallion come to earth with him? Furthermore, how did it find its way into his army backpack? None of the other treasures left Mangonel. The troll's gold and the Merlin's bag had stayed behind; why hadn't the medallion? This was just one more unanswered mystery concerning that hidden land. Perhaps he would never know the answer. Then again, maybe it was a sign that someday he would return to that strange place, and the medallion would be the key to the journey.

Dictionary—Chapter 24

Align: *To bring something into line or into its correct position*

Amazing: *Outstandingly good*

Amid: *Within, surrounded by things or people*

Apprehensive: *Fearful, worried*

Capable: *Able to do something well*

Coincide: *Happening at the same time*

Devastation: *Widespread damage*

Disastrous: *Completely unsuccessful*

Doom: *A dreadful fate*

Dreariness: *Dull and gloomy*

Fathom: *To understand something, usually something mysterious*

Igloo: *An ice structure built and used by Eskimos*

Immediate: *At this moment, right away*

Innermost: *A most central location*

Logical: *Sensible and factual approach*

Loomed: *About to happen*

Manipulating: *To control or influence somebody in an ingenious or devious way*

Ominous: *Threatening*

Omission: *Something left out*

Overwhelming: *Something so large it is difficult to comprehend the proportions*

Perpendicular: *At right angles, perfectly vertical*

Persist: *Keep trying, again and again*

Random: *Without a pattern or regularity*

Ranging: *A number of different things that belong to the same category*

Recover: *To get something back*

Rediscover: *To find something for a second or third time*

Relentless: *Never slacking, always at the same punishing level*

Scattered: *Spread around in different locations and away from each other*

Sheer: *A vertical drop-off*

Uncomfortable: *Feeling awkward or uneasy*

Vivid: *Very bright, extremely clear*

AUTHOR BIOGRAPHY

Jack Scherm was born in Cincinnati, Ohio. He and his five siblings resided in Kenwood until 1960, when his father was transferred to Toms River, New Jersey. After graduating from high school, he joined the US Navy. Following his four years of active service, he returned to New Jersey and has been there ever since. Although he never truly enjoyed writing, he ironically obtained employment writing and reviewing contracts. The experience blossomed into a love of the written word.

Upon retirement Jack was requested to preserve the original bedtime stories he concocted for his two boys. Years later, at the ripe old age of sixty-five, he took the request seriously. *The Kingdom of Mangonel* is the result. Jack is presently working on a sequel, *The Land beyond the Kingdom*. Jack and his wife of thirty-seven years continue to reside in and enjoy the Jersey shore.